Aces Wild

Also by Erica S. Perl

When Life Gives You O.J.

Vintage Veronica

Erica S. Perl

Aces Wild

A Yearling Book

 Published in the United States by Yearling, an imprint of Random House Children's Books, a division of Random House LLC, a Penguin Random House Company, New York. Originally published in hardcover in the United States by Alfred A. Knopf, an imprint of Random House Children's Books, New York, in 2013.

Grateful acknowledgment is made to Warner/Chappell Music for permission to reprint an excerpt from "Plant a Radish," by Tom Jones and Harvey Schmidt, from *The Fantasticks*.

Visit us on the Web!
randomhousekids.com

Educators and librarians, for a variety of teaching tools, visit us at RHTeachersLibrarians.com

The Library of Congress has cataloged the hardcover edition of this work as follows:
Perl, Erica S.
Aces wild / Erica S. Perl.—1st ed.
p. cm.
Summary: Eleven-year-old Zelly Fried's parents will not allow her to have a slumber party until she teaches her mischievous puppy, Ace, to behave, but with Grandpa Ace around, nothing is ever simple.
ISBN 978-0-307-93172-6 (trade) — ISBN 978-0-375-97104-4 (lib. bdg.) —
ISBN 978-0-307-97547-8 (ebook)
[1. Dogs—Training—Fiction. 2. Family life—Vermont—Fiction. 3. Grandfathers—Fiction. 4. Jews—United States—Fiction. 5. Slumber parties—Fiction. 6. Vermont—Fiction.] I. Title.
PZ7.P3163Ace 2013 [Fic]—dc23 2012023335

ISBN 978-0-307-93173-3 (pbk.)

Printed in the United States of America
10 9 8 7 6 5 4 3 2 1
First Yearling Edition 2015

Random House Children's Books supports the First Amendment and celebrates the right to read.

To "Ace's kids"

CHAPTER 1

"A-ce! Ace?"

I shook a box of dog biscuits. The sound never failed to produce the skittering noise of toenails on wood floors, and always resulted in my puppy hurling his whole body—from his long flapping ears to his short stump of a tail—straight at me.

Shake-a-shake-a-shake-a. "Aaaa-aace!"

Nothing.

Don't panic, I told myself. But how could I not? I had spent my entire eleven years trying to get a dog, and now—*poof!*—I'd lost him.

In the hall closet, I found a jumble of boots, but no sign of my spaniel mix's small freckled snout. Calling his name, I wandered through the house, opening doors, looking under furniture, and glancing outside in hopes of seeing a furry brown and white streak race past.

Through the kitchen window, I could see my mom raking leaves. It was only the second week in October, but already it seemed like everyone was talking about snow and trying to predict when the first flakes would fall. I waved frantically to get her attention, which resulted in her making the *Just a sec* sign, patting the air with one of her gloved hands. The car was gone, so I figured my dad was out at the store getting more salt or sand or other snow-busting materials. This being our family's first winter in Vermont, my parents weren't taking any chances.

Could Dad have taken my puppy with him? No way. Ace had had too many accidents in the car for that to happen. I had already checked every possible spot upstairs, and I was starting to feel pinpricks of worry. It was strange enough waking up and not finding Ace standing over me, chewing his beloved squeaky-toy banana (which I won for him at the Champlain Valley Fair) inches from my nose. But it was truly bizarre not to find him in any of his next-favorite spots: on my little brother Sam's bed, or on my parents' bed, or in the sunny spot on the bath mat. Ace's own dog bed was empty, but that was no surprise. He seemed to view the fuzzy green rectangle as his mortal enemy, so his only contact with it was full-on attack mode, shaking it from side to side until I tried to take it away, at which point the game would change to keep-away.

There was no way to explain it. My puppy was just plain *gone*.

The front door opened, and my mom blew in with a loud "Wow! It's nippy out there!" She stomped her boots on the mat and stripped her gloves off.

"Mom, have you seen Ace?" I asked her.

"Ace-the-dog or Ace-the-grandpa?" she asked.

I held up the box of dog biscuits.

"Right," said my mom. "Ace-the-dog."

I never would've named Ace Ace if I had realized this would be the standard response to the question. The thing is, when I got Ace-the-dog, my grandpa—who is, yes, also called Ace—claimed he was going to retire the name. According to him, the nickname Ace represented his old self: the loud, kvetchy, tell-you-what-to-do-y guy he left behind when he had a heart attack (and almost died). The plan was that Ace-the-dog would be the only Ace. Ace-the-grandpa would be just plain Grandpa.

Unfortunately, with Ace-the-grandpa around, things don't usually go as planned.

"I haven't seen Ace-the-dog yet this morning," said my mom. "Come to think of it, I haven't seen either Ace."

There was one place left to check: Ace-the-grandpa's room. A no-dogs-allowed zone if ever there was one. Ace's door was shut, so it seemed unlikely, but I needed to rule it out. Cautiously, I knocked.

"Grandpa?" I said, cringing in anticipation of Ace's booming "WHA?"

But it didn't come. This was starting to feel like an old episode of *The Twilight Zone*, Ace's second-favorite show after *Star Trek*. Had aliens come in the night and taken *both* Aces? I pushed the thought out of my mind and knocked again, louder this time.

"Ace?" I tried.

Bupkis, as Ace would say. No response.

Ace-the-grandpa was probably sleeping. That is, I hoped he was sleeping. Ever since his heart attack, I was a lot more nervous that something bad was going to happen to him. Every coughing fit that forced him to sit down made my heart race like I was going to have a heart attack of my own. But each time he turned out to be fine, I would tell myself, *See?* Still, I couldn't seem to stop worrying in the first place. So getting no answer at Ace's door did not feel good at all. Even his usually annoying response of yelling "WHA?" would have been reassuring.

I was turning to go back to the kitchen when I heard a very soft whining noise: *hrrnnnnn*.

Now, that sound, I'd know anywhere.

"Ace!" I exclaimed happily. Slowly, I turned the handle and opened the door a crack.

"Ewwwwwwwww!"

The telltale smell hit me first. Holding my nose, I stumbled in, fumbling for the light switch, and stepped in something squishy.

Click. I found the switch. The ceiling light came on, revealing:

Yup, that's what I stepped in.

And, yup, another mushy pile right next to it.

And, yup, total chaos in all directions.

My mom often says that my room looks like a cyclone hit it, which is just plain not true. But Ace's room actually did. Several issues of *Golf Digest* magazine had been shredded, and clothing was everywhere, like a basket of laundry had been tossed in a blender with the cover off. For good measure, there was a big dark stain on the throw rug beside Ace-the-grandpa's bed. The bed itself was, thankfully, the only thing that appeared to be undisturbed.

And guess who was wagging his whole body excitedly? *You're here!* his happy expression and thumping stubby tail seemed to say. *It's about time! Now the party can really begin!* He was standing over a pair of Ace-the-grandpa's beloved golf shoes. Which looked like maybe his favorite pair, the ones with the tassels. Or maybe it was another pair, which, thanks to a good gnawing, now looked tasseled.

"Oh no! Acey . . . ," I groaned, covering my face with one hand.

Yup. Good news! I found Ace-the-dog.

The bad news?

Ace-the-grandpa—assuming he hadn't been abducted by aliens—was going to have another heart attack when he saw this disaster.

Or kill me. Or both.

CHAPTER 2

"I don't get it," I told my mom as we tackled Ace's floor together. She had already cleaned off my slippers and Ace's newly "tasseled" golf shoes and put them outside to "air out"—though, this being Vermont, I was pretty sure that meant "freeze stiff." She was on her knees with a spray bottle of Nature's Miracle, which my dad said we should get stock in since Ace-the-dog joined our family. "How did he end up in Grandpa's room?"

"Beats me," she said, wadding up more paper towels. "I let Ace out last night right before I turned in."

"Weird," I told her. "Grandpa wouldn't have let him in. And I'm pretty sure Ace was in here for a long time. I mean, seriously," I added. "It usually takes him a while to make this much of a mess."

My mom nodded sympathetically. Ace seemed to see it as

his personal quest to attack, destroy, and pee on everything he came into contact with. From what I'd read in *Your New Puppy*, a lot of this could just be his puppy energy. Though when something like this happened, I got nervous that my parents might lose their patience. And might conclude that Ace was Too Much Trouble after all—as they had always insisted a dog would be—and start looking for a new home for him. A girl in my class last year said her mom did that when her dad got stationed overseas.

"Maybe he woke up early and drank all the coffee," suggested my mom. This was a reference to a cartoon my dad had put on the refrigerator. It showed a couple of dogs lining up at a coffee dispenser, and underneath it said: "How nervous little dogs prepare for their day." My dad changed it so it now says: "How Ace prepares for his day."

I smiled at the thought of Ace sitting at the table with a big, steaming mug of coffee. It was pretty nice of my mom to not freak out about Ace's latest disaster, so it helped me breathe a little easier too.

Still, I jumped when I heard the front door slam.

"OY YOY YOY! YOU COULD FREEZE YOUR TUCHES OFF ON A DAY LIKE THIS. LYNN? NATE? WHERE IS EVERYBODY?" My mom thinks Ace is loud because he's hard of hearing. But I've noticed that he hears just fine when he wants to. I think he just likes to be loud.

"In here, Dad," yelled my mom. "I'll be right there. Stand by the woodstove and warm up a minute."

"Great," I said, feeling my flood of relief that Ace was okay drain out of me like water from a bathtub. "Well, it's been nice knowing you."

"Relax, Zelly," said my mom. Everyone calls me Zelly instead of my real name, Zelda. Well, almost everyone.

"HIYA, KID," said Ace, shuffling in to join us. Ace jumped up happily and attacked Ace's boots. "HIYA, DOGGELAH."

"Dad, how many times do I have to tell you," scolded my mom. "Leave your boots by the stove when you come in."

"Hi, Grandpa," I said. I call him that to get him back for *kid*. He prefers to be called Ace. Or Your Honor, because he used to be a judge and often acts like he still is.

"SO NU? YOU'RE HAVING MY ROOM FUMIGATED?"

"Ah, no, Dad," said my mom, getting up. "Ace just had a little accident."

"I'm sorry, Grandpa," I said. "I promise I'll do a better job. . . ." My voice trailed off and I winced, waiting for the lecture to begin.

Instead, Ace started chuckling. He leaned over and cupped his hand around Ace's shaggy chocolate-brown ears. "YOU LITTLE PISHER. YOU MESHUGGE MUTT. VEY IZ MIR, WHAT ARE WE GOING TO DO WITH YOU!"

I looked at him curiously. Yiddish, I expected. But cheerfulness in the face of disaster was a decidedly un-Ace-like reaction. It wasn't that Ace had no sense of humor. Far from it. In addition to collecting rubber bands and golf balls, Ace had an unparalleled collection of corny jokes. But when Ace meant business, that was another story. And this was definitely a situation that called for him to dust off one of his

"In all my years of experience on the bench"—meaning as a judge—speeches.

"You're not . . . mad?" I asked cautiously.

"I MUST BE MAD OR I WOULDN'T BE HERE," said Ace, giving me his *Guess who I'm quoting* wink. When I didn't hazard a guess, he barked, "LEWIS CARROLL. *ALICE'S ADVENTURES IN WONDERLAND*. COME ON, KID, THINK."

"Wait, you're really not angry?"

"AT WHO?"

"Well, uh, me," I said.

"YOU MADE A MESS ON MY FLOOR?" Ace asked.

"No, Grandpa. Just, I mean, he's my dog."

Ace knew only too well that Ace was my dog. In fact, if it weren't for him, I wouldn't have Ace. Ace-the-grandpa had dreamed up this ridiculous plan involving, of all things, a "practice dog" made out of an old plastic orange juice jug. I had to walk O.J., and feed him, and clean up after him (don't ask) all summer until I was pretty convinced that I had made the biggest mistake of my life. And then Ace had his heart attack. And then he recovered (and promised to stop being so "Ace"). And then my parents, to my complete and total surprise, gave me my puppy as an early eleventh-birthday present.

"RIGHT," said Ace, switching gears and putting on his usual Ace-itude. "HE IS YOUR DOG AND YOUR RESPONSIBILITY. WHICH MEANS IT IS YOUR JOB TO KEEP HIM *IN* CONTROL AND *OUT* OF TROUBLE."

I was about to respond and argue—even though my dad always says that arguing with Ace is like talking to a brick wall—that unless I kept Ace-the-dog on a leash 24-7, there was no way of guaranteeing he wouldn't get into trouble. But before I could, my mom said, "Dad, what time did you get up this morning?"

"I DON'T KNOW. EIGHT-THIRTY? NINE?"

"And when did you go out?"

"WHAT IS THIS, THE INQUISITION?"

My mom frowned at him. "Dad, I have been out front raking leaves for the last hour or more, but I never saw you leave. You must have gone out before any of us were even up. Is there any chance Ace got into your room this morning and you closed him in by accident when you went out?"

Ace smiled broadly, like he had just told a riddle and my mom was trying to figure it out. "NONE WHATSOEVER."

My mom looked at me, then at Ace again. "Okay," she said, "I'll bite. How can you be so sure?"

"NOT THAT IT'S ANY OF YOUR BUSINESS," said Ace. "BUT I WENT OUT TO VISIT A FRIEND LAST NIGHT. IT GOT LATE, SO WE JUST DECIDED TO HAVE A . . . WHADDAYA CALL IT, KID?"

"A sleepover?" I asked.

"THERE YOU GO!" said Ace.

"Out to visit . . . who exactly?" asked my mom.

"YOU KNOW PAULA," said Ace. "FROM THE Y."

Paula had come to our house for dinner the week before. Ace had met her at a class his doctor made him take after his heart attack. It was called Heart-Healthy Seniors, and Ace complained all the way there the first time he went. He said things like "FOR THIS I NEED A CLASS?"

Then he met Paula. He went early to the second class.

"Dad," said my mom cautiously, "don't you think it's a little, well, soon? I mean, you only met Paula, what? Three weeks ago?"

"FOUR," said Ace. "BUT WHO'S COUNTING?"

"Plus," I added, in case Ace had forgotten, "Bubbles hasn't even been gone a year yet." The whole reason we had moved to Vermont and Ace had moved in with us was that my grandma, who we called Bubbles, wasn't alive anymore. I could tell that Bubbles wouldn't have liked Paula, who had a really phony smile. And she wore too much makeup and clothes that Bubbles never would have worn, like a teal velour sweatshirt with matching pants. She also had a super-curly gray perm, so every time I heard Paula, I'd think poodle.

Both my mom and Ace turned when I spoke, looking startled, like they had forgotten I was even there.

"Sweetie," said my mom. "Why don't you go see if your dad's back yet?"

"But I haven't finished cleaning up after Ace."

"I'll take care of it," she said.

"Okay," I said quickly, before she could change her mind. "C'mon, boy."

As soon as Ace and I had left the room, my mom shut the door. I was just refilling Ace's water bowl when the front door opened and, with a gust of freezing wind, my dad came in. Wagging excitedly, Ace made a dash for his boots.

"Whoo-whee!" said my dad, shuffling across the floor

with the groceries, then peeling Ace off him. "It's not fit out there for man or beast." Like my mom and Ace and practically every other grown-up in Vermont, my dad was incapable of coming inside without commenting loudly about the weather.

"I found Ace," I told my dad.

"Didn't realize you lost him, but okay. Where was Mr. Puppy-School-Dropout?"

"Hey! Ace didn't drop out. He took a leave of absence," I said, reminding Dad of what he'd said to cheer me up when it happened. After all, nobody likes to get a note saying: "At this time, Ace is too wild to participate in dog obedience class without disrupting the group."

"Right," said my dad. "Sorry," he told Ace, who took the apology as an invitation to renew his boot attack.

"Ace, quit it!" I said, pulling him off and holding him by his collar.

Just then, Sam walked in, rubbing his eyes. As usual, he was wearing his ratty old Luke Skywalker bathrobe. On his left cheek was a big round red mark, in the shape of the button eye on Susie, the stuffed whale he used as a pillow every night. Susie had been blue when Sam got her as a baby, but after six years of near-constant use, she was a grimy gray schmatte with a single straggly piece of yarn left as her spout. Sam refused to part with her, though, and schlepped her around with him to school and back every single day.

"Where's Mom?" asked Sam.

"Ace's room," I replied.

From down the hall, through the closed door, came the unmistakable sound of Ace's booming voice saying "NOT THAT IT'S ANY OF YOUR BUSINESS!" again.

"Is Grandpa in trouble?" whispered Sam.

"Sounds like it," said my dad. "What'd I miss?"

I shrugged, trying to act like it was no big deal. "Ace messed up Grandpa's room. Plus Grandpa had a sleepover, and Mom's not that happy about it."

Sam's eyes got big. "Because he had a sleepover on a school night?" he asked.

I snorted. "Sam, duh. Today's Sunday."

"Oh yeah," said Sam. "Hey, I hope he didn't forget."

"Forget what?"

"Ace said I could go to the Y with him on Sunday to watch his friend Margie's Yoda class."

"Margie's . . . what?" I asked. Sam's obsession with *Star Wars* didn't surprise me. But if someone Ace's age was equally obsessed, that would be another story.

"Yoda class," repeated Sam. "She teaches it at the Y."

My dad and I exchanged confused looks. "What exactly does 'Yoda class' involve, Sam?" asked my dad.

"What involved, mmm . . . I know not!" croaked Sam, jumping at the opportunity to do his Yoda voice.

Just then, Ace stomped into the kitchen. He was wearing the same clothes as before, though he had changed from his wet snow boots into a pair of un-chewed-on golf shoes. Mom lets him wear them in the house as long as he removes the spikes from the bottom of them first.

Across the room, Ace-the-dog sat up and gave a low murmur of interest, though he nervously eyed the rolled-up foam mat Ace was carrying under his arm. Rolled-up things, like the *New York Times Magazine* often wielded by Ace-the-grandpa, were not Ace-the-dog's friends. Ace went to the junk drawer by the phone, pulled out his emergency stash of rubber bands, and began securing the rolled-up foam mat with them.

"SAMMY! NU?" he said without looking up. "YOU READY?"

Sam scrambled to his feet as if he'd been invited to board the *Millennium Falcon*. "I've just got to get my lightsaber!" he cried, running upstairs.

Just then, I realized what Sam must have thought. Sam regularly got things wrong. Like thinking that the police "under-arrested" bad guys. Or singing along to Dad's favorite song like this: "I'll never leave your pizza burning. . . ."

"Margie teaches . . . *yoga?*" I guessed.

"BIKRAM YOGA," corrected Ace. "A HUNDRED AND FIVE DEGREES IN THE SHADE."

"You're taking a hot yoga class?" asked my dad.

"OF COURSE NOT. WHAT KIND OF MESHUGGENER DO YOU THINK I AM?"

"But Sam said you were taking him to the Y for Margie's Yoda—I mean *yoga*—class."

"RIGHT. FOR ME, IT'S MORE OF A SPECTATOR SPORT. IT'S LIKE A SHVITZ, BUT WITH ENTERTAINMENT."

"What's a shvitz?" I asked.

"It's like a sauna," said my mom, who had just walked in carrying a laundry basket. "Who's Margie?" she asked.

"I JUST GOT DONE WITH THE TWENTY QUESTIONS. ASK THE KID."

"She teaches yoga," I reported.

"Really," said my mom. "Oh, speaking of which, Dad, I forgot to tell you. This morning, before you got back, your friend Arlene called. Something about tickets to a show?"

"GOOD. GOOD," said Ace dismissively, putting on his coat, scarf, and a hat he liked to call his ice-fishing hat. That was because it was identical to his lucky fishing hat, except it was a thicker material. My dad claimed he would eat both of Ace's hats if Ace ever went near a frozen body of water, much less ice fishing. Ace's coat was huge and dark green and had a name too. He called it The Baxter State. I had no idea why.

"SAMMY, BUS STOP," Ace yelled up the stairs before heading outside to stand on the corner.

A few minutes later, Sam scrambled after him, his bathrobe belt trailing like a tail from under his down parka. On silent paws, Ace crept out from under the table and expertly snagged it off him without Sam noticing. However, in my almost two months as a puppy owner, I had learned a few tricks of my own. I grabbed a spray bottle from the counter. One well-aimed squirt of water and the belt would be mine. *Future Skywalker meltdown averted.*

Or so I thought.

The whole thing happened kind of fast. I had the end of

the belt in one hand and the spray bottle in the other. But the next minute, I had both ends of the belt, and Ace was running around with the bottle in his mouth, chewing it like a squeaky toy. As he chomped, his sharp puppy teeth must have pricked tiny holes in it, because icy cold water was spraying everywhere like a sprinkler.

"Zelly, hey! Stop him!" yelled my dad, holding up his newspaper to shield himself.

"I'm trying! Ace, drop! Drop!" I yelled. Pleased to have my attention, Ace paraded in and out of the kitchen, then turned and charged straight down the hall toward—*oh no*—Ace-the-grandpa's room again. As I went to try and disarm him, I overheard my dad say to my mom, "Did I hear correctly? Ace is up to three girlfriends now?"

Three girlfriends? I thought. *Ace? Grandpas aren't supposed to have girlfriends at all. Much less three.* I froze, listening for my mom to tell him he was wrong.

Instead, my mom chuckled softly. "That we know of," she said.

CHAPTER 3

"Three girlfriends?" said my best friend, Allie, when I told her on the way to school the next morning.

"That we know of," I added ruefully.

I didn't mention the sleepover part. Sleepovers were a sore spot for me. It seemed like every weekend since sixth grade began, there was another sleepover party that Allie was invited to and I wasn't.

In New York, all my friends lived in tiny apartments like me, so nobody I knew had sleepovers—the kind you see in movies with pillow fights and toenail painting and lots of girls. In Vermont, people lived in houses and had rec rooms, and it was a different story. Sleepovers happened and they were important. Or so I'd come to understand, since—truth be told—I hadn't been invited to many sleepovers. Any, in fact, except for at Allie's. Allie said this was just because I hadn't had one of my own yet. According to Allie, who had it on good authority from her big sister, Julia, once you had one, every girl you invited would invite you back. Until then, I was out of luck.

"Zelly! Hey, Zelly, wait up!"

I turned at the sound of my name and saw a giant blue marshmallow with legs sprinting down the street toward us.

"Hey, Jeremy," I called back, watching my breath freeze in the air. I wasn't wearing a real coat because nobody in middle school in Vermont seemed to wear a real coat, on account of the fact that it wasn't, technically, winter yet because there was no snow. Well, almost nobody.

With one hand on his head, an oversized down parka, and an even more oversized backpack, Jeremy Fagel was unmistakable, even from a distance. Jeremy was what Ace liked to call a mensch, which is Yiddish for a nice guy who's also kind of a dork.

Dorky how? Well, for example, on the first day of sixth grade, otherwise known as the first day of middle school, Jeremy showed up at my house with his braces, glasses, wavy hair, and buckteeth . . . and the brightest, greenest T-shirt on the planet.

"BEWARE OF THE GREEN MONSTER?" I read out loud. "Like on *Sesame Street*?"

"Green monSTAH," he corrected me. "Fenway Park. You know, where the Red Sox play?"

"Oh," I said. I guessed that would go over okay. But when I looked down, yikes. Jeremy's white-and-red-striped socks were pulled all the way up to his knees. As soon as we got outside, I said, "No offense, but maybe you should fix your socks."

"Fix them?" Jeremy looked down. "Why, are they broken?" he joked.

"Jeremy!"

"What?"

Was he really that clueless? I bunched up my own socks to demonstrate. "Like this," I said. "Scooch them down a little. So they don't go all the way up to your knees?"

"But they're kneesocks," protested Jeremy.

We walked on in silence from there, though out of the corner of my eye I could see Jeremy glancing downward. At the corner, he bent down to retie his sneaker even though I hadn't noticed it was untied. It looked like maybe he was adjusting his socks while he was down there, which made me relieved, but then I noticed something else.

"What's that on your head?" I asked.

Jeremy was still bent over his shoe, but one hand flew up and he squinted at me through his glasses.

"You mean my kipa?" he said. It sounded like *KEY-pa*.

"I guess," I said.

"What about it?"

"It's just— You don't wear one." By which I also meant that I had never seen a boy in Vermont wear one. Possibly because Jeremy was the only Jewish boy in Vermont I knew, except for Sam.

"I don't always. In the summer, it's too hot." It was typical of Jeremy to see this in purely practical terms.

I leaned in to examine it. The yarmulke looked like someone's grandma had knitted it. It had Hebrew letters and a blue and red and white design that looked familiar.

"Is that . . . a Red Sox yarmulke?" I asked.

"Yup," said Jeremy proudly, tilting his head.

"And are you wearing . . . barrettes?"

"Yeah. To keep it on. Why?" He stood up.

I stared at him, dumbfounded. I wasn't sure which would get him teased worse: the yarmulke or the barrettes.

When we got to school, we stood around outside awhile. I introduced Jeremy to some of the other sixth-grade girls, who nodded politely, then went right on talking like he didn't exist. Some of them compared cell phones they got over the summer. Some whispered and giggled about the boys.

Then, all of a sudden, Megan O'Malley yelled, "Hey, Brendan!" Her brother, who was in fifth grade, came running over. Megan pointed at Jeremy and said, "Check out what he's wearing!"

Brendan stared.

Oh no, I thought. *Here it comes. What was it going to be, the kipa or the barrettes? Or the goofy kneesocks, for that matter.*

"Green monstah, yeah!" said Brendan. "Were you there when they won the series?"

"Uh-huh," said Jeremy.

By the time the bell rang, Jeremy was telling stories about catching foul balls in the alley behind Fenway Park, and he had all the boys eating out of his hand too. At lunch, Jeremy waved at me from across the lunchroom and came and sat at my table, even though he was the only boy. And he didn't get teased for that, either!

It felt really strange, watching Jeremy go off after lunch to play wall ball with Scott Cooper and the rest of the boys. On the one hand, I was happy for Jeremy. If anyone deserved to make friends, it was him. But it didn't seem fair, somehow, that I'd had to put up with so much teasing when I was new and Jeremy hadn't had to put up with any. I cringed, remembering how Nicky Benoit had made fun of my name and got all the boys in the cafeteria laughing about it. Meanwhile, by day two, Jeremy was firmly established at the boys' lunch table and wall ball game, as if he'd been here forever. Red Sox yarmulke still clipped to his wavy hair, braces and glasses and the whole megilla, as Ace would say, with nobody—not even nasty old Nicky—saying anything about it.

And it wasn't just that first week. Here it was, six weeks later, and Jeremy was still walking to school with me, and nobody ever said anything. No other boy in our grade walked to school with a girl, unless she was his little sister and he had to!

"Your grandpa has *three* girlfriends?" asked Jeremy once I caught him up on the story about Ace.

"That we know of," repeated Allie, smirking.

"All right already," I said in protest. It was one thing for me to say it, but that didn't make it okay for her to say it. "You guys can't tell anyone. Promise," I said, staring straight at Allie.

"Okay, okay," said Allie, looking insulted that I would even suggest she might blab.

"It's nuts," I continued. "Number one, my grandma hasn't even been gone a year yet. Number two, he just had a heart attack. And number three, he's old. It's totally inappropriate."

I ticked these off on my fingers while Allie nodded sympathetically.

"Why?" asked Jeremy. He kicked a horse chestnut down the sidewalk like a soccer ball, shooting a pass to me but missing by a mile. Allie and I looked at each other and shook our heads. Boys could be so dumb sometimes. Allie fished the horse chestnut out of a pile of leaves and started it rolling again.

"It just is!" I said. "He shouldn't have one girlfriend, much less three."

"Ever?" asked Jeremy, kicking the horse chestnut back to Allie.

"Yes! Because of Zelly's grandma," explained Allie. She passed our "ball" to me, and I kicked it back to her.

"Exactly," I said. I looked up at the sky, which I do out of habit whenever I think about Bubbles. I don't exactly believe in heaven, but for some reason I always picture her up in the sky sitting on a fluffy white cloud. She's wearing her paint-spattered overalls and she's picking little tufts of the clouds and eating them like cotton candy. Thinking about her, I wondered if she spent a lot of time looking down at us. And, if she did, was she mad at Ace for forgetting all about her and running around trying to find someone new? Or several someones.

It was hard to imagine Bubbles mad. She was always smiling, always laughing. Always making presents and painting paintings and baking goodies for other people. She took care of everyone around her—that's just how she was. Bustling around her kitchen whenever we visited, even after she got sick, stocking treats like homemade rugelach and Barton's Twin Almond Kisses for me and Sam. Long after we got old enough to tell her what we liked and didn't like, she'd pull my mom to one side, asking, "Does he want cottage cheese? Nem a bissel. I have melon, does she want melon? A schtickl lemon cake, maybe?" And if there was only one piece of cantaloupe—her favorite—there was no way she'd eat a single bite herself. She put all of us first: me, Sam, my parents, and, of course, Ace.

I was pretty sure that if anything would make her mad, it would be this. I mean, who could blame her? After all her years giving all that love and kindness and generosity to Ace, this was the ultimate betrayal. *I haven't forgotten about you,* I told Bubbles silently, hoping this would cheer her up. *And I never will.*

"So, he shouldn't be allowed to get married again?" asked Jeremy.

"He's not getting married!"

"You know what I mean. He should be alone forever?"

"No," I said. "I mean, maybe. I don't know!" I said in exasperation. Jeremy was a lot like Ace sometimes. He loved to debate things, and he had a way of twisting things around so I wasn't so sure of what side I was on. "You just don't get it," I told him. "You'd feel the same way if it was your grandpa." It was true, but I didn't want to say any more because I didn't want Jeremy to feel sad. His grandparents were no longer around.

"Plus it's just weird," added Allie. "Old people kissing and stuff? Eww!"

"Allie!" I hadn't even thought about that. "Yuck!" I added, making a face and trying to push the idea out of my mind. "Can we talk about something else, please?"

"Okay," said Jeremy agreeably, trying to snag the horse chestnut back from Allie with his foot. "Hey, did I tell you I got my date?"

"You're going on a date? With who?" I asked, raising an eyebrow. *First Ace, and now Jeremy?*

"My bar mitzvah date," explained Jeremy. "They assigned them at Hebrew school yesterday."

"Oooh! Zelly, you should have a bar mitzvah," said Allie. "Julia went to one. She said it was the best party ever. There was a chocolate fountain, and a DJ, and everything!"

"She can't," Jeremy informed her.

"Why not?" asked Allie.

"Well, for starters, she's not a boy. Girls have *bat* mitzvahs. Also, Zelly doesn't go to Hebrew school. Plus they give out dates about two years in advance."

"I could if I started going to Hebrew school," I said.

"Are you going to?" asked Jeremy. "You should do it! I could help you catch up, if you wanted. You could come check it out this Sunday morning. You could come too," he said to Allie generously. "I mean, if you're curious."

"I can't," said Allie. "I'll be at Simone's."

"You will?" I asked, feeling my heart sink. "Sleepover?"

"Uh-huh. It's her birthday. Sorry—I'd rather hang out with you, Zelly, but I already said yes."

"It's okay," I said, trying to sound nonchalant. Simone Matthews was in Allie's homeroom, not mine, but still. She usually sat with both of us at lunch. I even traded her a blueberry mini-muffin for a speckled banana once—which was a really bad deal—just to be nice.

"Hey, you should ask your parents if you can have a sleepover next weekend!" suggested Allie.

"Yeah, maybe," I said. That minimal encouragement was all Allie needed. She started jumping up and down.

"Do it! Do it! Do it!"

"Okay, okay. I said maybe. It's not like I haven't asked before."

"This time they'll say yes," insisted Allie. "I can totally see it. I'm psychic, you know."

"Oh yeah?" said Jeremy. "What are they serving for hot lunch today?"

Allie stared at Jeremy. Then she stopped walking and scrunched up her eyes tight, deep in concentration.

"Turkey tacos," she finally said.

Jeremy shook his head. "It's pizza."

Allie shrugged. "Nope, my psychic energy is definitely picking up turkey tacos."

"Maybe you're so psychic you're predicting tomorrow's lunch," said Jeremy. "According to my mom and the menu in the newspaper, today's pizza day."

"We shall see," said Allie mysteriously. "Zelly, you believe me, don't you?"

"Sure," I said, because she is my best friend. But then I kind of forgot about it when we got to school. Until lunchtime rolled around and I got in line to pay for my milk. Standing there, I noticed that the board announcing the hot lunch said:

TURKEY TACOS

I got a spooky little chill looking at it. Allie couldn't really be psychic. *Or could she?* I guess I must have looked funny because the cashier said, "Were you hoping for pizza? We'll have it tomorrow."

Allie had a huge grin on her face. "You see!" she said, pointing triumphantly to Kristin Garrett's hot lunch tray when I sat down next to her. "Now you have to ask them about the sleepover when you get home!" said Allie. "They're going to say yes!"

"What sleepover?" asked Jenny Hood.

"Zelly's going to have a sleepover," announced Allie.

"Allie!" I said.

"You are?" asked Megan O'Malley, who was Jenny's best friend. "When is it? Can I come?"

"Sure! But, I mean, it's not a done deal or anything. I still have to—"

Megan glazed over before I finished speaking. She turned to Jenny. "Are you bringing your bathing suit to Simone's? I heard her dad works at the Radisson and is going to take us swimming there." She paused, then added, "At *midnight*."

"No WAY!" yelled Jenny. Allie shrieked with excitement, and Megan swacked her to keep the lunch ladies from coming over.

"I'm definitely having a sleepover," I found myself saying, louder than I meant to. My heart was beating fast, but I told myself it was okay since Allie had predicted my parents would say yes. "I just need to figure out when. I mean, my family's pretty busy."

"Well, you better invite me," said Megan.

"And me," said Jenny.

"I promise," I told them. Then I went to throw away my trash so I wouldn't have to hear another word about Simone and her sensational sleepover plans.

As Allie knew, my parents had surprised me by giving me Ace-the-dog as an early birthday present. What Allie didn't know is that when they did, they made one thing clear: This was it. No asking for anything else for a really, really long time. So even though I wanted all sorts of other things too—like a cell phone and contact lenses and pierced ears—I knew there was no way. But a sleepover party didn't seem like such a big thing to ask for. Right? Everybody had parties. For Sam's birthday in August, my parents took him and a whole carload of his friends to Sally's Pizza and let them get so many soda refills that, well, put it this way: the backseat of our car now smells like dryer sheets. And it's not just because of my dog!

That evening, my parents offered to take me and Sam out to Bove's for dinner. The dryer sheet smell in the backseat reminded me that I had something to ask them. Hoping that Allie's psychic success was not limited to lunch menus, I brought up the idea of me having a sleepover as casually as I could.

"Absolutely not!" said my mom.

"Why not?" I asked. I tried to catch my dad's eye in the rearview mirror to see if I could enlist his help, but when he glanced up, I could tell that he was going to be on my mom's side.

"I think you know why," said my mom. "Three letters: *A-C-E*."

"Grandpa can stay in his room while my friends are over."

"Ha!" My dad laughed out loud at that. "Not that Ace, Zellyboo. The four-legged one."

"We know he's just a puppy," said my mom. "But with all the accidents and destruction and willfulness . . . You saw what he did to Ace's room yesterday. Your dad and I feel like it's not such a good idea to entertain yet."

"You wouldn't have to entertain," I promised. "It would just be my friends. They don't care."

"But we do," said my mom. "Look, sooner or later, he'll be trained. And then we'll see."

"We'll see when? If I do it, can I have one?"

"If you do what, can you what?" asked my dad.

"What's on second," offered Sam eagerly. Ever since Ace taught him this corny old comedy routine called "Who's on

First?" Sam looks for any opportunity to launch into it. So does Ace.

"Sam!" I said. I took a deep breath and tried again. "If I train Ace, can I please have a sleepover?"

"Wellllll," said my mom, looking at my dad.

"We're reasonable people," said my dad. "Write up a proposal."

I couldn't help it. A little groan escaped.

"What?" said my dad.

"Everybody else's parents just say yes or no. Why do I always have to write up a proposal?"

"Would you rather have a no?" asked my dad.

"No!" I practically shouted.

Fine, I'd write up a proposal.

The way writing up a proposal works in my family is, you have to make a list of the reasons something should go your way. Occasionally, it works. Like when I got them to move lights-out thirty minutes later in the summer than during the school year, or when I got them to agree to let me and Sam each get a pack of sugarless gum at the grocery store if we both help out at the checkout and don't whine for junk food the whole trip.

More often, though, it doesn't work. Like when I made a proposal about going to sleepaway camp with Allie.

This one *had* to work. But how? The last time I did a proposal, Jeremy suggested I ask Ace to help me. "That way, you'll have an Ace up your sleeve. Get it?" And he laughed his horsey laugh, with all his braces showing.

At the time, I ignored him. But now his words came back to me. *An Ace up my sleeve might be just what I need.* Ace was a former courtroom lawyer and a retired judge. Ace could out-argue anyone, as far as I knew, and he had an answer for everything. Plus he loved being asked for his opinion. Fine—what did I have to lose?

So I asked Ace for a judicial consult, and when he agreed, I showed him what I had written:

Proposal for Training Ace
by Zelly Fried

1. I will take Ace to dog-training classes.
2. I will train Ace to behave and not act wild.
3. Ace will take a test on his training.
4. If Ace passes, I will get to have a sleepover party and invite up to eight girls.

Ace looked it over, then ordered, "YOU WANT EIGHT? PUT SIXTEEN."

"Grandpa! My parents will never let me have sixteen girls sleep over," I told him.

"EXACTLY!" said Ace. "YOU GOTTA HAGGLE. SIXTEEN'LL GET YOU EIGHT, YOU WATCH."

"Why can't I just ask for eight?"

"DOUBLE IT," he ordered. "JUST DO IT, DON'T ASK ME WHY."

There was no way sixteen was going to fly, but after some back-and-forth, I agreed to change *eight* to *twelve*.

"YOU WATCH. TWELVE'LL GET YOU SIX," insisted Ace. "IF IT DOESN'T, I OWE YOU A NICKEL."

"Maybe you could be there when I present this to them," I suggested. "You could be the judge on the case?"

Ace shook his head. "NO CAN DO, KID. CONFLICT OF INTEREST."

I must have looked confused, because he explained. "A JUDGE HAS TO RECUSE HIMSELF IF HE HELPED ONE OF THE SIDES PREPARE THE CASE. OR IF HE'S ROOTING FOR ONE OF THE SIDES TO WIN."

"You are?" I asked.

Instead of answering, Ace asked, "YOU EVER HEAR THE ONE ABOUT SHLOMO THE SCHLEMIEL? HE PACKED A SUITCASE TO GO TO THE COURTHOUSE?"

I had heard all of Ace's jokes before, but this time I shook my head and let him tell it again.

"SO SHLOMO'S GOT HIS SUITCASE AND HE'S HEADED OUT THE DOOR. 'WHERE ARE YOU GOING?' ASKS HIS WIFE. 'I'M TAKING MY CASE TO COURT,' SAYS SHLOMO. NEXT MORNING, SHLOMO'S HEADED OUT THE DOOR AGAIN, AND HE'S GOT THE SUITCASE, BUT THIS TIME HE'S GOT A LADDER TOO. 'WHERE ARE YOU GOING NOW?' ASKS SHLOMO'S WIFE. 'I'M TAKING MY CASE TO A HIGHER COURT.' THAT DAY, IT GETS LATER AND LATER, AND STILL NO SHLOMO. FINALLY, AT ELEVEN O'CLOCK AT

NIGHT, HE SHOWS UP. NO SUITCASE, NO LADDER, JUST A COAT HANGER. 'WHAT HAPPENED?' DEMANDS HIS WIFE. AND SHLOMO SAYS . . ."

"I lost my suit," I chimed in with him.

CHAPTER 4

"So, how exactly are you going to train the holy terrier?" asked my dad. He was reading my proposal while scratching Ace behind his floppy ears, which seemed like a good sign to me. "Are they actually going to let him reenroll after his 'leave of absence'?"

"I think so. He's ready to go back," I said. "And so am I." I had looked it up ahead of time because Ace said I should come "armed with information." "A new session of classes starts this Thursday at seven," I continued. "I just need you or mom to go with me, like last time." This was a rule of the dog-training program. Kids ten and up could attend and learn how to train their dogs, but you had to have a grown-up in the room. My dad had been looking for a job when we tried to take the class the first time, so he sat in the corner, pen in hand, reading the want ads the whole time.

"Thursdays at seven?" said my mom. "That's actually a little tricky, sweetie. Your dad's teaching Tuesday and Thursday nights now, remember?"

"Oh, right," I said. In New York, my dad had worked in a research lab, but the job he ended up getting in Vermont included the chance to teach night school students. "Okay, well, you could come," I said.

"Maybe," said my mom, "but Sam goes to bed at seven-thirty. Who's going to put him to bed and stay with him?"

"Grandpa?" I suggested.

My mom and dad both smiled indulgently at that idea. Ace and Sam got along great, but on many occasions Ace had proved himself a total failure at the key objective of babysitting Sam: actually putting him to bed. Once, my parents had taken me to see a play at the Flynn Theater and brought me home so late *I* fell asleep in the car—only to find Ace snoring in a chair and Sam watching *Saturday Night Live*.

"What about if Ace went with you?" asked my mom.

"He kind of has to go with me," I said, playing dumb. "How else are they going to train him?"

"Ha-ha," said my mom. "I think you know who I'm talking about. The other Ace. The two-legged one."

"Yeah, no thanks."

"He'd just have to sit there and read the newspaper, like I did," said my dad. "He's a pro at that. Seriously, Zelly, why not?"

"Um, lots of reasons," I said, my heart starting to beat faster. "I mean, for starters, isn't he kind of, um, too old?" I didn't want to say the other reasons, like the fact that he's also too loud, too weird, and *way* too embarrassing.

"Well, they say some dogs are too old for new tricks," said my dad. "But in Ace's case, I wouldn't be surprised if he proved them wrong."

I looked from my dad to my mom. "Do I have to?" I asked.

"Of course not," said my mom. She took the proposal from my dad and looked it over. "But if you really want to have a slumber party, it seems like you've made a good case for it."

"So, that's your answer? If I want to have a sleepover, I have to take Ace to class and take Grandpa with me?"

"Nate?" asked my mom, passing the proposal back to my dad.

"Yes," said my dad. "And Ace has to pass the obedience test. Ace-the-dog, that is. If all that happens, you can have some of your friends sleep over." He glanced down at what I had written one more time. "But, Zelly?"

"Hmmm?"

"Twelve girls is too many," said my dad.

"Eight?" I asked, trying not to smile. I clicked the ballpoint pen Ace gave me for "sealing the deal."

"Six," said my dad.

"Yesss!" said Allie when I told her the next morning on the way to school. "See! I told you so! Ohmygosh, it's gonna be awesome! And you have to invite everyone—seriously, everyone. I mean, not *everyone*, but everyone who's anyone—"

"Zelly, hey! Wait up!"

Allie and I hung out at the corner while Jeremy looked both ways before crossing and shuffled up the block dragging his huge backpack. It looked like one of the straps had broken.

"I'll tell you the rest later," I whispered.

"Why?" Allie whispered back.

"Just 'cause," I said. There were some things about Jeremy that couldn't easily be explained. Like the fact that he always invited me to do stuff with his other friends, even if it meant I'd be the only girl. Even though he'd probably understand why I wanted an all-girls party, I didn't want to hurt his feelings by talking about it in front of him. Lots of boys don't care about stuff like that, but Jeremy isn't exactly like lots of boys.

So it wasn't until Allie came over to my house after school that I could tell her the details. "They said yes, but here's the deal," I said, rummaging around for Ace's leash while he cantered and twirled in place, ready to explode with excitement for his afternoon walk.

"Yeah?" she asked.

"I have to take Ace to dog obedience class first. And pass a test. Before I can have the party."

"So?" said Allie. "You trained dogs all last summer!"

"I *walked* dogs," I said. "It's not the same thing. Plus Ace has already been kicked out of class once, remember? For being hopelessly untrainable."

"Oh. Right," said Allie.

"But that's not the worst part," I added.

"PLANT A RADISH, GET A RADISH, NOT A BRUSSELS SPROUT . . . ," sang Ace as he wandered into the kitchen and pulled open the junk drawer.

"O-kay," I said, giving Allie a look but knowing full well . . .

" . . . THAT'S WHY I LIKE VEGETABLES, YOU KNOW WHAT THEY'RE ABOUT!"

. . . that Ace was incapable of stopping once he started.

"FANTASTIC!" Ace crowed, pulling a screwdriver out of the drawer and holding it up triumphantly.

"It's . . . okay. For a screwdriver."

"NOT *FANTASTIC*, KID. *FANTASTICKS*! REMEMBER, YOUR GRANDMA AND I CAME TO NEW YORK FOR A VISIT AND TOOK YOU?"

"Oh, right," I said, feeling a pang as living in New York and still having Bubbles around came rushing back to me. It felt like a million years and five minutes ago all at the same time. "It's a Broadway show," I told Allie, pushing the memory aside.

"OFF-BROADWAY," corrected Ace. "THE LONGEST-RUNNING OFF-BROADWAY SHOW IN HISTORY. YOUR GRANDMA STILL HAS THE TICKET STUBS. I MEAN—" Ace looked flustered for a moment. I hated it when he messed up and talked about her like she was still alive, even though I sometimes did too. "SHE KEPT THINGS LIKE THAT. WHADDAYA-CALL-ITS, MEMENTOS," he said.

"Cool," said Allie.

Before Ace could mistake her politeness for actual interest,

I said, "C'mon, Allie!" and opened the door. With one big yank, Ace-the-dog dragged both of us out into the freezing cold.

Outside, I told her the rest of the sleepover requirements, including the part about six girls, not twelve, and the part about having Ace-the-grandpa go to dog-training class with me. Meanwhile, Ace-the-dog bounded as far as his retractable leash would let him, hopping over piles of leaves like a rabbit. Then he dropped into a squat and froze for a moment.

"Is there something wrong with him?" asked Allie.

"Yes, obviously!" I said. "And you know that in a group of people like that, he's going to be extra loud and bossy and opinionated and—"

"Not your grandpa Ace," interrupted Allie. "This one. He's a boy dog, right? Isn't he supposed to go like one?"

"Oh, right." I had wondered the same thing myself. But I looked it up, so I knew what to tell her. "All puppies pee that way. When he gets a little older, when he's ready, he'll just start lifting his leg and peeing on trees and stuff."

"Huh," said Allie. And then, "So, are you going to do it?"

"What, lift my leg and pee on trees?"

Allie burst out laughing at the idea, and I lifted my leg to make her laugh harder. I knew what she meant, though, so when we caught our breath, I said, "I don't know."

Allie was silent as Ace pulled on his leash, desperate to keep moving and sniffing, hoping to find a soggy pizza crust or some other treasure. I noticed a discarded tennis ball, threw it, and watched Ace chase after it, then lunge into piles of leaves, trying to figure out where it had disappeared.

"If it were me, I would," Allie said.

"You so wouldn't."

"Would too," protested Allie.

"You're just saying that because you want me to have a sleepover."

"Am not! I mean, I do, but that's not why. Besides, I like your grandpa. He's so . . . funny."

"Oh, he's funny all right," I said.

Allie and I dragged Ace back to the house and stood by the kitchen woodstove, trying to warm up.

"You girls hungry?" asked my dad, who was peeling carrots at the sink. Ever since moving to Vermont, my parents had gotten much more health-food-y than they were before. My dad had even started reading cookbooks with strange names like *Moosewood* and *Horn of the Moon*. In New York he was more of a takeout-Chinese kind of dad.

"No thanks," we both said at the same time.

"If you're not in the mood for carrots, I've got some fabulous golden raisins from City Market. Nature's candy!"

I gave Allie a quick *Told you we should've gone to your house* look. My dad's not such a bad cook, but Allie's family has much better snacks.

Just then, I heard my mom's voice coming from the mudroom.

"Dad, we need to talk about this," she said.

"ALL RIGHT ALREADY," said Ace. "RIGHT NOW I'M LATE FOR MERENGUE."

Ace marched into the kitchen. My mom followed him. Ace grunted and returned to the mudroom.

"Merengue?" my mom asked my dad, frowning.

"Well," reasoned my dad, lining up several carrots on a cutting board, "if Jewish grandmas can play mah-jongg, why can't Jewish grandpas dance the merengue?"

"That's not the point, Nate, and you know it," said my mom.

Ace reemerged wearing the Baxter State, a bright red scarf, and his ice-fishing hat.

My mom was waiting for him.

"What happened to Heart-Healthy Seniors, Dad?" she asked.

"WHA?"

My mom lifted one of the earflaps on his hat and repeated her question.

"I ASK YOU, IF MY HEART WASN'T HEALTHY, WOULD I BE ABLE TO DO THIS?"

Ace raised his hands, palms up, and began to make these little shuffling steps. "YAI-DAI-DAI-YAI-DAI-DAI . . . ," he sang as he shuffled. He looked like Tevye in *Fiddler on the Roof*.

"That's great, Dad," said my mom. "I just wonder if we should maybe check with Dr. Walters before you hit the dance floor."

Still shuffling, Ace put his thumb on his nose, wiggled his fingers, and went *thhhhhhft!* "I'LL HAVE YOU KNOW THAT I'M IN GOOD HANDS. MY MERENGUE INSTRUCTOR, LINDA, IS IN THE MEDICAL PROFESSION."

"Oh?" said my mom pointedly. "Is she a cardiologist?"

Ace shook his head. "CLOSE," he said. "SHE'S A DENTAL HYGIENIST."

"Dad! It's not the same—"

"MARILYNN, ENOUGH. VEY IZ MIR!"

"That's Yiddish," I explained to Allie. "It means—"

"It's like *oy vey*, right?" asked Allie.

My parents and Ace all stared at her.

"YOU SURE YOU'RE NOT JEWISH?" said Ace.

Allie shook her head and blushed.

Ace shrugged. "LOVE TO STAY AND CHAT," he said, "BUT MERENGUE WAITS FOR NO MAN. HASTA LA VISTA, SHALOM, AND GOOD NIGHT."

And with that, he shuffled out the door.

CHAPTER 5

Beep! Beep!

"I'm coming!" I yelled, even though I knew Ace-the-grandpa couldn't hear me from the car. Class was starting in twenty minutes, and I was running around gathering up Ace-the-dog's things, as directed by a handout my dad had printed when he signed me and Ace up. It said to bring:

1. The puppy
2. A leash
3. A mat
4. A water bowl
5. A puppy "pacifier" or favorite toy
6. Plenty of treats

I had the puppy and he was attached to the leash. I had also found an old bath mat, a plastic bowl, and Ace's squeaky banana, and I was going to fill a small bag with Cheerios, one of Ace's favorite things. Except we seemed to be out of them.

Beeeeep!!!

"Hold on!" I muttered, hurrying to pull out boxes of cereal and granola, trying to find a new box of Cheerios. Raisin Bran, Uncle Sam—another Ace favorite—and Kix, yes, yes, yes. But no Cheerios. I finally gave up and reached for the Kix, but Ace, seeing an opportunity, jumped up on me, sending me—

"Whoa!"

Wham!

I fell backward, landing on the floor. The box hit the floor too, spilling cereal in all directions. *Ouch!* I rubbed my elbow. Ace, thrilled to find me at eye level, thoughtfully focused his licking on my face rather than the cereal-strewn floor.

"Ooh!" whispered Sam, who had just padded in, wearing his Luke Skywalker bathrobe over his pajamas and carrying his disgusting Susie-the-schmatte. You knew something was truly gross if Ace-the-dog had no interest in putting it in his mouth. Sam stared at me on the floor, surrounded by tiny cereal balls. "The universe!" he said in awe.

"Yeah, space. The final frontier," I joked, grabbing a handful of Kix off the floor and shoving them into a plastic baggie. Ace-the-dog would not care. In fact, he seemed to prefer food that came from the floor. Before Ace-the-grandpa could lean on the horn again and before Ace-the-dog could eat the whole galaxy, I stood up, yanked on the leash, and pulled my dog out the front door, into the waiting car.

When we arrived at the puppy kindergarten parking lot, Ace started hopping around, looking out the window nervously. I could tell he knew where we were: the scene of the crime. The place he got thrown out of the last time we tried to take classes. I felt jumpy too. Other people were getting out of cars with their dogs. The dogs looked, well, obedient. Maybe my dad had signed me up for the wrong class? Maybe the Thursday class wasn't for beginners? A Great Dane got out of the car parked next to us and stared calmly at Ace, who was scraping the window with his paws frantically, like he thought he could claw his way through the glass. *Kid*, the giant dog seemed to say, *you are seriously out of your league*.

My spirits lifted, though, when we went inside. There were all kinds of dogs: big ones, small ones, fluffy ones, and smooth ones, and several of them turned out to be puppies—even the huge Great Dane. A yellow Lab puppy approached Ace and bowed down in Ace's favorite *Wanna play?* position, chin between front paws, tail high and wagging. But before Ace could face off with him, the other puppy's owner pulled him away from us, saying "Sorry! Sorry!" over her shoulder.

Even though I had made sure Ace peed before bringing him inside, I chose a spot by the door so I could make a hasty exit if he started to squat. I looked across the room to verify that Ace-the-grandpa was still in the folding chair I had left him in—

No Ace.

No chair, for that matter.

Just then, I noticed that about halfway across the room

Ace was walking determinedly in my direction, dragging the chair, which he had not bothered to refold. This was creating a high-pitched metal *screeeeeech*ing noise, so now every dog ear in the room was perked up high. I ran over to him, Ace at my heels.

"Grandpa, what are you doing?"

"I'M COMING OVER TO SIT WITH YOU."

"Grandpa, that's not—" I lowered my voice and glanced around. "That's not necessary. You can just sit and read your newspaper. Like Dad did."

"EXACTLY!" said Ace. "THAT'S WHY I'M OVER HERE."

I was about to tell him that my dad's lack of participation wasn't the reason Ace flunked out last time, but just then a short lady walked in carrying a clipboard. She had orange hair and glasses on the top of her head. I was hugely relieved to see that she was not the dog trainer who was in charge last time. If anyone needed a clean slate, it was Ace. Trotting next to the lady, matching her hair color almost perfectly, was a fluffy Pomeranian.

"Rosie, go lie down," the lady said. The little dog immediately obeyed. Ace cocked his head like this reaction made absolutely no sense to him whatsoever. Clearly, this little furry creature was from another planet entirely.

"I'm Delores Wright," said the lady, addressing the group. "I'd like to welcome all of you to Puppy Training 101! Many people call this puppy kindergarten, and while it will be fun, it is also a lot of work. For this reason, I take attendance every week, and I'll need every participant to practice between classes and get here on time. At the end of the session, I will administer a training test. Any questions?"

She looked around the room. I shot Ace a *No questions!* look, which earned me a raised eyebrow. "Good, let's get started," she continued. "When I call your name, please raise your hand. Kathy Keller and Georgie?"

"Here!" The woman who had pulled her dog away from Ace raised her hand and waved. "Mark Johnson and Romeo?" continued Mrs. Wright, looking around the room. A large man with a very tiny black dog nodded and lifted his hand. Mrs. Wright kept going, and I almost thought she'd finished when she called out, "Zelda Fried and . . . Ace?"

A rumble of amusement went around the room. I looked at Ace-the-grandpa. Both of us had our hands in the air. "Is one of you . . . Ace?" asked Mrs. Wright, wrinkling her forehead as she peered over her clipboard. She looked from me to Ace-the-grandpa. Ace-the-dog cocked his head to one side.

"He's Ace," I said. "I'm Zelly. I'm the one who's doing the class. It's my dog."

"Okay, what's your puppy's name?"

"Ace," I said quietly.

"Sorry, I can't hear you," said Mrs. Wright. "Can everyone please quiet their dogs? Now say that again."

I sighed. "Ace," I said, louder.

Mrs. Wright looked confused. "I thought you said he was Ace?" she said, pointing her pen at Ace.

"He is. They both are," I told her. "It's a long story," I added.

Mrs. Wright stared at us for a minute. Then she sighed and checked my name off her list. She put down the clipboard and began to talk about what she called "training the trainer." Ace immediately began to doze in his folding chair. Bubbles always used to say that one of his great talents was his ability to fall asleep anywhere. However, I was pretty sure that Mrs. Wright was not going to be impressed.

"Ace!" I whispered quietly. Then louder. "Ace!"

"I see one of our students is already ready for lesson two," said Mrs. Wright.

I looked over and saw she was staring right at . . . Ace. The dog, that is. Ace's floppy ears were as perky as they were capable of being, and his head was cocked keenly to one side as he stared at me with rapt attention.

"I'm sorry," I said.

"Don't be. Your pup clearly knows his name, which is a skill we'll be focusing on next week, when we play the Name Game. Give him a treat, dear."

I dug in my pocket and produced a Kix. I tossed it in the air, and Ace handily caught it.

"No, no, you can't do that," scolded Mrs. Wright. "You need to mark the behavior. That way he understands that the reward is specific to what he did right. Call his name, and when he gives you his attention, mark it by telling him he's a good dog and delivering the treat."

"Okay," I said. "Ace?"

But now Ace was ignoring me and scratching his ear furiously. I tried again. "Ace?" *Scritch, scritch, scritch.*

Now the whole class was watching me. To make sure I got Ace's attention, I used a much louder voice. "ACE?!"

"HUH? WHA—?" Startled, Ace-the-grandpa sprang to life in his chair, causing Ace-the-dog to stop scratching and turn to stare at him.

"Not you," I told him.

"NOT WHO?"

"Not you. Ace," I said.

"I AM ACE," said Ace.

"Not you Ace," I repeated firmly. "Him Ace." I half expected Ace to try to launch into "Who's on First?" right then and there. All I would've had to do was say "I don't know" and I'm sure Ace would've answered "Third base!" right on cue.

"OH. THAT ACE," said Ace, sounding disappointed, like he wished he was the one getting a treat.

"Ruff!" barked Ace, like *Enough already. Shouldn't I be getting a treat?*

"See? He responded to his name. Mark it!" instructed Mrs. Wright.

"Good boy!" I threw a Kix at Ace-the-dog.

"No, no, him," said Mrs. Wright.

"Okay," I said, tossing cereal at Ace-the-grandpa.

Mrs. Wright stared at me. "No, dear," she said. "He should provide the treat. Because when he said the name, he got the dog's attention."

"Oh," I said.

CHAPTER 6

As we pulled into the parking lot the next week, I decided to do what my math teacher, Mr. Tortoni, always did before we'd start a new unit. He'd put on this ridiculous hat with the letters *R* and *E* written on it, which he called his RE-cap. Then he'd summarize the entire lesson to make sure we understood all the material we'd covered. Even without a hat, I figured it might be a good idea before we went inside to summarize for Ace what I had talked about the whole way there.

"Tonight's class is called the Name Game, remember?" I said. "I practiced with Ace and got him ready. So all you have to do is stay in your chair while I do the class with him. You don't participate."

"RIGHT! SIT. STAY. GOT IT."

"Good," I said, almost slipping and saying *Good boy*.

Think positive, I thought. Me. My class. Ace on the side,

watching, listening if he wanted, but, above all, behaving himself.

Unlike last week.

It sounded too good to be true. But, like my dad said, old dogs could sometimes learn new tricks . . . right? Of course, the only actual old dog I knew well was Bridget, the beagle that belonged to the Stanleys, our next-door neighbors. Poor old Bridgie had to be about a hundred in dog years. She couldn't see or hear very well, but she was still the best-trained dog I knew. She could walk politely on a leash, sit at any opportunity, lie down if you even thought about asking her to, and roll over for a tummy scratch. But these were old tricks for her. Could Bridget learn new tricks? I wasn't so sure.

We walked into class just before it was scheduled to start. Ace pulled out his *New York Times* crossword puzzle, and I felt a huge wave of relief. This wasn't a new trick for him. But if he succeeded at the more challenging task of not participating at all—not commenting loudly on the proceedings or getting into the middle of them—he could have all the treats in my treat sack. Which, tonight, contained cut-up pieces of Hebrew National salami—one of Ace's favorites. One of Ace-the-grandpa's favorites too.

Mrs. Wright started us off in a circle, standing with our dogs. One at a time, she called people into the center, instructing them to let out the leash and allow their dogs to wander before calling their names. A lady with a schnauzer went first. Her dog took a few steps in the direction of the circle, and Mrs. Wright nodded.

"Mika!" said the lady. The dog turned immediately and looked back at her.

"Good, great, mark it!" ordered Mrs. Wright. "Who'd like to go next?"

The man with the Great Dane got up to try. His puppy seemed thrilled at the opportunity to stretch her long legs and galloped away from him the moment he let out her leash.

"Lady? Lady!" he tried. The dog's ears perked up, but she didn't turn. You could almost see her thinking through it like a math problem. *Name equals treat, maybe, but treat equals sitting down and not romping. Hmmmm . . .* She took another couple of giant steps in the direction of Ace, who was pulling determinedly on his leash to meet her halfway.

"Ace, stop it," I said.

"WHAT?" came from behind me.

"Not you," I said, feeling my face get hot as I tried to push Ace's wiggling bottom down into a sitting position.

"Quiet, everyone!" called Mrs. Wright. "Let's try again. This time, show the treat first, then pocket it. Let your dog know there's something in it for her but she's gotta pay attention to you."

The man did as he was told, and it seemed to work. The dog's head moved, following his hand as he repocketed the treat. But when he tried again, the same thing happened as before.

"I know their names mean something to you," said Mrs. Wright, "but you have to remember that to your dogs they're just words until you teach them otherwise. Let me show you something." She turned to me. "Sweetie, do you mind if I borrow Ace for a minute?"

"Oh, um, no, go ahead." I held out the leash to her. Instead of taking it, she walked past me.

"Would you mind helping us with a little demonstration?" she asked.

Ace-the-grandpa looked up, startled. Perhaps he had even been dozing. I saw him doing the math, just like the Great Dane had. *Request from teacher equals participation and attention, but earlier request from grandchild equals no participation and . . .*

"WHY NOT?" said Ace.

The two of them conferred briefly. Then, to my surprise, Ace followed Mrs. Wright into the center of the circle. *What could she possibly want with Ace?* I wondered. The only one who seemed more unhappy about this arrangement than me was Rosie, Mrs. Wright's Pomeranian. Rosie was either the world's laziest dog or even better trained than Bridget. She usually spent the entire class lying next to Mrs. Wright's purse and watching, but when Ace-the-grandpa entered the ring, Rosie sprang to her feet and began to fidget.

"Rosie, down," said Mrs. Wright coolly.

Instantly, Rosie crumpled to the floor and resumed her usual posture. But her eyes never left Mrs. Wright.

"Now, for this demonstration," said Mrs. Wright, "I'm going to need a volunteer. Let's see. . . . How about you, Zelly?"

This was a classic teacher trick, often used by Mr. Tortoni: call on the one person not raising her hand.

"Your neighbor can watch your dog," added Mrs. Wright. "This will just take a moment."

Since it didn't seem like I had a choice, I handed Ace's leash to the lady standing next to me and walked to the center of the circle to join Ace and Mrs. Wright.

"Okay, go ahead," said Mrs. Wright to Ace.

"SCHLEMIEL!" said Ace in his booming voice. Several people laughed.

"Sorry?" I said.

"SCHLEMIEL," repeated Ace, smiling.

"Grandpa, stop it," I whispered. I was pretty sure a schlemiel was a weirdo or a loser, but I didn't know why he was saying it again and again. Especially in front of all these people.

"SCHLEMIEL!" insisted Ace. He reached into his pocket and pulled out half a roll of butterscotch Life Savers. Holding the candy, he walked over and gestured to a folding chair Mrs. Wright had just set up. "SCHLEMIEL, SCHLEMIEL!" he said emphatically.

"Okay, well, schlemiel to you too," I said, suddenly understanding. I sat down in the chair.

"MAZEL TOV!" said Ace. I looked up and saw that Ace's hand was right in front of my face, holding a somewhat linty Life Saver.

"No thanks," I said.

"TAKE IT. I'M MARKING YOU."

"Fine." I took the Life Saver, but I didn't eat it.

"Great job, Zelly!" said Mrs. Wright, beaming. "Let's all give Zelly and Ace a big round of applause."

Ace flapped his hand modestly, like this was unnecessary. But he didn't return to his seat. Instead, he started lecturing the group.

"I USED YIDDISH TO MAKE A POINT," he announced. "TO A DOG, ENGLISH, YIDDISH—IT'S ALL THE SAME. IT'S GIBBERISH!"

"Exactly," said Mrs. Wright.

"HE DOESN'T KNOW A *HEEL* FROM A *SCHLEMIEL*."

"Precisely," she added.

"HE'S IN A FOREIGN COUNTRY. DOESN'T KNOW THE LANGUAGE. HE'S THE NEW KID."

Like I was, I thought, looking down at Ace. He was wagging his tail and smiling expectantly, as if he hoped some scrumptious morsel might magically materialize. New was good by him. Tasty, even! Clearly, Ace-the-dog was the Jeremy kind of new kid.

"BEFORE THE DOG CAN LEARN, THE MASTER HAS TO."

"I love that," said Mrs. Wright. "That's it exactly! So, now let's all try playing the Name Game. But as you are calling your dog, try to put yourself in his shoes. Er, so to speak."

"IT'S JUST FASCINATING," said Ace as we left class.

"What?"

"THE EVOLUTION OF ATTITUDES," said Ace. "WHEN I WAS A LITTLE PISHER, DISCIPLINE—OF CHILDREN, MUCH LESS ANIMALS—INVOLVED A STERN VOICE AND A STEADY HAND."

I had never thought about Ace being a kid. He had been a grandpa my whole life. "Were you ever the new kid?" I asked.

"SURE," he said. "WHEN I FIRST CAME OVER. AND AGAIN WHEN MY FAMILY MOVED FROM THE LOWER EAST SIDE TO BROOKLYN. BUT YOU KNOW WHEN I REALLY FELT LIKE THE NEW KID? WHEN YOUR GRANDMOTHER AND I MOVED TO VERMONT."

I had to laugh at that. "But, Grandpa, you were, like, *old*," I said.

"WATCH IT, KID!" protested Ace.

"I mean you were a grown-up," I explained. I remembered seeing the movers put their things in a truck when I was little. At the time, I thought they were going to live in the truck. I was jealous because it had a ramp up the back. I thought it would make a great slide, and I wished I could live in their new "house" too.

"YOUR GRANDMOTHER WANTED TO MOVE HERE, NOT ME," said Ace. "I WOULD HAVE BEEN PERFECTLY HAPPY STAYING IN BROOKLYN, WHERE I KNEW WHERE TO GET EVERYTHING I LIKED."

"Dad says he's found a place to get bagels here that are acceptable," I told him.

"PFFFT!" Ace made a face to express his strong disagreement with my dad's optimism on the bagel front. "YOU WANT TO TALK UNACCEPTABLE, YOU SHOULD SEE WHAT PASSES FOR CHINESE FOOD HERE. FEH! BUT YOU KNOW WHAT YOUR GRANDMOTHER SAID?"

"What?"

"SHE SAID, 'DON'T BE AFRAID OF CHANGE.' AND

SHE WAS RIGHT. IT'S HARD, BUT IT JUST TAKES TIME."

I nodded. My mom said something like that when we moved. But half a year had gone by already, and I still felt like the new kid. *How much time?* I wanted to ask.

"SHE WOULD'VE FOUND THIS DOG-TRAINING BUSINESS INTERESTING. SHE HAD A REAL THING FOR ANIMALS."

"Bubbles?" I asked, surprised. "I don't remember you guys ever having any pets."

Ace shook his head. "NOT PETS. SHE DIDN'T BELIEVE IN KEEPING ANIMALS. SAID IT WOULD BREAK THEIR SPIRITS. BUT YOU REMEMBER HERMAN?"

"No . . . Wait, yes," I said as a whisper of a memory drifted back to me. "Behind The Farm?" I asked, picturing the house where Bubbles and Ace had lived when Bubbles was still alive.

"EXACTLY," he said. "THERE HAD TO BE A DOZEN OF THEM, ALL LIVING OFF FIELD MICE BEFORE YOUR GRANDMOTHER AND I MOVED IN. ALL OF THEM STARTED SHOWING UP, NIGHT AFTER NIGHT, GETTING FED BETTER AT THE BACK GATE THAN I WAS AT THE TABLE! 'IT'S JUST ONE CAT' IS WHAT SHE'D SAY. SHE WAS A SMART COOKIE, YOUR GRANDMOTHER." Ace smiled proudly. "HOW COULD I BEGRUDGE HER FEEDING ONE STRAY CAT?"

"I almost forgot about Herman," I told Ace. All of the cats had some white parts and some spots, so they seemed like brothers and sisters, which they probably were. When I would visit Ace and Bubbles, I would chase them, but I never got close enough to pet them, much less catch them. Bubbles could, though, so she'd occasionally fetch "Herman" and hold him or her still for me. A memory swam back to me just then: me feeding tuna fish out of a can to one, while Bubbles beamed down at me and petted my hair like *I* was a cat. I liked this idea so much that I got on all fours and ate some tuna fish myself, right alongside the real cat. Bubbles laughed but she didn't stop me. She just stroked my hair and called me her favorite kitty of all.

The surprise of the memory felt like finding money under your pillow even though you didn't remember losing a tooth. And then poking your tongue around your mouth and discovering the hole. It made me happy and sad and scared all at once. In time, would I lose everything I had of Bubbles? Ace hadn't, which was good, but he had known her longer. Was a little over eleven years—some of which didn't even count because I was just a baby—enough time to seal up those memories forever, like those prehistoric bugs trapped in amber they have at the natural history museum in Manhattan?

Just then, I remembered something I had been wanting to ask Ace. "Who said that thing?"

"WHAT THING?"

"You know, the thing you said in class. About how before the dog can learn, the master has to."

"OH, *THAT* THING." Ace looked surprised, then pleased. "I DID," he said proudly.

CHAPTER 7

"Ace . . . Ace . . . ACE!"

"Ace . . . Come on, Acey."

"A-ACE! Hey, Ace!"

"Ace! Attaboy! Good boy!"

For two days, I practiced the Name Game with Ace. He was excellent at responding to his name inside the house, especially in the kitchen, where he knew the snacks were readily available. He was pretty good on the sidewalk or in the backyard. And he was downright terrible if another dog—or a cat, squirrel, or tennis ball—was anywhere in the vicinity.

By Sunday, all Ace seemed to have learned was that his name meant "food." He hadn't gotten any better at doing what came after his name, like dropping things, sitting, or—his most challenging task—staying. Although, he was getting much better at coming when he was called. Too good, in fact: at least twice, my dad had yelled, "Ace!" from the kitchen, meaning Grandpa, only to find Ace-the-dog hurtling toward him at breakneck speed.

"You couldn't have gone with Spot or Snoopy or something?" he asked.

"Or O.J.," added my mom.

"There was only supposed to be one Ace," I reminded him. "If anyone should be using another name, it's Grandpa."

"I hear George Foreman has five sons and he named them all George Foreman," said my dad, gesturing to his beloved indoor grilling machine. "I suppose I should be grateful we only have two Aces."

"There's four aces in a deck," announced Sam. He held up one to demonstrate, then placed it on top of a card tower he was building at the kitchen table. Ace had started teaching him card games recently, and he liked to show off his new information. "I could be Ace and you could be Ace too, Dad, and then we'd have four Aces."

Four Aces! I pictured the four aces from a deck of cards. Except each one was walking around, with little feet and hands, plus glasses, bushy eyebrows, and a big nose. Like Groucho Marx . . . or a certain grandpa of mine. More cards joined them, all aces, until I had imagined an army of the card-men. They looked like something out of *Alice in Wonderland*, which Ace used to read to me when I was much too little to understand any of it. Rectangular and flat, yet broad-bellied and balding, the cards were all blowing their noses and hitching up their pants and arguing with each other . . . and there were so many of them, sort of like all those Herman-the-cats.

My dad's eyes were wide. He must have had the same

thought. "No way," he said firmly. "Two Aces are plenty, thank you very much."

"One Ace is behaving better, don't you think?" I asked pointedly. "He definitely knows his name, right?"

"Ye-es," said my dad slowly, examining the handle of the spatula he was holding. It appeared to have been chewed on. "It would just be nice if he mastered a couple of other tricks."

"He will!"

"HE WILL IF YOU PRACTICE," said Ace, who had wandered into the kitchen.

"I *have* been practicing!"

Ace shrugged. "THERE'S PRACTICING AND THEN THERE'S PRACTICING."

"It's how you get there," said Sam matter-of-factly, adding another card to his tower. I looked at him, confused, but his eyes were on the structure in front of him. Sometimes, if Sam was concentrating hard, he said things that made no sense because he was responding to a conversation that had ended a while earlier.

"EXACTLY," said Ace. I could feel a round of "Who's on First?" coming on.

"What's how you get—"

"CARNEGIE HALL!" said Sam and Ace together. Sam laughed so hard he knocked his card tower down. Cards fell all over the table and floor. Ace dove under the table on cue. I grabbed him by the collar before he could destroy another deck.

"I'm not so sure Carnegie Hall is ready for Ace," said my

dad, shaking his head. I could tell he was having the same thought I was: Ace-the-dog performing his world-famous sit-stay onstage for an audience. I guess that was funny for my dad, because he was sort of smiling, but for me it was an exciting thought. *Maybe, with practice, he'll be so well behaved and obedient that* Mrs. *Wright will ask me to demonstrate for the rest of the class.* I pictured Ace-the-dog wearing a tuxedo, bowing low to thunderous applause. I imagined myself at his side, curtsying and catching the long-stemmed roses people were throwing.

"Maybe he'll get so well behaved, he won't even have to take the test," I said. "Because Mrs. Wright will know he'll ace it."

"He'll *Ace* it!" laughed Sam. "Get it, Zelly?"

"Yeah, I get it," I said. I picked up Ace and cradled him in my arms like a baby. "The question is, do *you* get it? Do you, sweetie? I hear they have really yummy dog biscuits at Carnegie Hall."

Ace licked my nose at the sound of that.

Fine, I'll practice, I thought. But I had a lot of homework on Monday, and then on Tuesday I forgot, so on Wednesday I decided to do an extra-long session to get Ace ready for Thursday's class. I figured I'd walk him up to Redstone Campus, where there'd be plenty of distractions—students, other dogs, Frisbees—to test him so he could maybe break through to a new level of listening to me.

I went straight to the kitchen to pack up some dog treats and found Sam sitting at the kitchen table with his head buried in his arms. My mother was crouching next to him, one hand on his back.

"What's wrong?" I asked. "Is Grandpa . . . ?"

"Grandpa's fine," said my mom.

"It's all my fault!" said Sam, sitting up and revealing his tear-stained face.

"Sweetie, let's not start that again. What matters now is that you remember where you saw him last?"

"Saw who?" I asked, grabbing Ace's leash and pulling out a box of Cheerios before yelling in the direction of the stairs, "Aaaa-ace!"

Sam looked pained. His bottom lip trembled.

I turned sharply, realizing. "Where's Ace?" I asked.

"I was just twying to help," whispered Sam. When he got *weally* upset, Sam's *r*'s were the first thing to go. "I just took him out to pwactice," blubbered Sam. "To get him weady for . . ."

"Where's Ace?" I repeated, more firmly this time.

"Carnegie Hall," wailed Sam. He burst into tears again.

Just then, the phone rang. My mom let go of Sam and ran to get it. "Hello?" she said. "Yes. Yes, why? Oh my—okay. He's okay? All right, where is he now? I'll be right there."

"Did they find Ace?" I asked.

"Yes," she said distractedly, grabbing her keys off one of the hooks by the door and going into the mudroom for her coat. "He's been in a little car accident. I need to go pick him up," she called.

"What!" I said, alarmed.

"He's fine, everything's fine. It's just a fender bender, apparently. Stay here, okay? I'll be right back."

"Can I go with you?" I asked, following her.

"Zelly, I need you to stay here with Sam."

"But he's my dog!"

My mom looked at me, confused. Then she said, "Oh, honey. Not the dog. Your grandfather. Grandpa's been in a car accident."

"He's what?!"

"They said he's fine but the car's not drivable, so I need to go pick him up."

"Okay, but what about Ace? My Ace?"

"Zelly, he's got to be in the neighborhood. You and Sam should go out and look for him. I'll call your dad and tell him to come straight home. Make sure you're back before it starts to get dark. And if you don't find him by then, we'll call the animal shelter and see if maybe someone turned him in. Someone might call too—remember, he has our number on his tag."

"Yeah, I know. Okay."

Wearing my hoodie over my sweater, I trudged through the neighborhood shaking a box of dog biscuits and dragging my little brother.

"Hi, Zelly. Hi, Sam," called Mrs. Brownell, who was out walking her poodles, Maddy and Luna. All three of them were wearing jackets in various shades of pink. She pulled off her matching fuzzy pink earmuffs. "Where's Ace?"

"Actually, I was hoping maybe you'd seen him?"

"No," said Mrs. Brownell. "But if we do, we'll make sure he stays put." I didn't know how to tell her that if Ace knew how to stay put, we wouldn't be in this situation in the first place!

I offered dog biscuits to Maddy and Luna. Luna turned up her nose, then barked as Maddy devoured hers too. "We've spoiled Luna with those fancy Pupcat Bakery treats," said Mrs. Brownell, shaking her head. "Now she won't touch anything else."

Sam and I walked on, keeping an eye out for Ace.

"Ace! Acey! Come on, sweetie! A-ace," I called.

"I have a stick for you," added Sam.

Sam threw sticks at bushes and I didn't stop him, since one of Ace's favorite activities was to chase flying things of any kind. I kept hoping he'd come bounding out of the bushes, ears flapping, mouth open wide.

No such luck.

Sam fidgeted with the zipper on his jacket, eyes down, bottom lip in a permanent pout.

"Sam, stop potchke-ing with that," I ordered. "Come on, any idea where Ace might have gone?"

"No," admitted Sam.

"Well, I guess we'd better hop a bus for New York. Carnegie Hall, here we come," I said. Sam kicked me in frustration. "All right, okay, stop!" I said. "It's just, jeez, Sam, what were you thinking? You know you can't take him out without asking. What if he's gone for good?"

"He's not!" said Sam.

"You don't know that," I snapped. Sam could be so frustrating sometimes. He was big enough to do dumb stuff like letting my dog out. But he was too little to know that sometimes you don't get a do-over. Sometimes gone really means gone.

"Do too," insisted Sam. "I used the Force."

"Sam! That's just made up. It doesn't actually exist."

"Does too!" yelled Sam, starting to cry again. It didn't really seem fair for him to be so sad when he was the one who lost my dog. "That's how Jedis contwol stuff! Evwybody knows that!"

"All right, all right," I said—fighting the temptation to say *all wight*—and wiped his face with my sleeve. "Enough, okay? We'll find him."

When we got home again, Mom still wasn't back. I helped Sam peel off his wet socks and boots, and I sat him in front of the woodstove, which was still warm. I filled two mugs with milk, stuck them in the microwave, and pulled out the cocoa mix. Sam looked so sad I tossed him the bag of mini-marshmallows even though the cocoa wasn't ready yet. Then, remembering how Ace-the-grandpa had accidently locked Ace-the-dog in his room, I went down the hall, just to make sure.

No puddles. No chewed-up shoes. No Ace.

Just then, I heard the doorbell ring. Before I could make it back to the kitchen, I heard a man's voice, then Sam's. What was with that kid today? First, taking Ace out without asking, and now answering the door and letting strangers in while Mom and Dad were out? But as I walked in—*crash!*

I was pounced on by twenty pounds of wriggling, wiggling, wet, licking—

"Ace!" I cried, wrapping him up in a hug, then using his trailing leash to prevent him from licking my face off. My heart was beating with excitement and happiness, and all my frustration with Sam just melted away. Sometimes you don't get a do-over, but luckily sometimes you do!

Just then, I looked up and noticed that there were two men standing in our kitchen and they were both wearing dark blue police uniforms. And all of Ace's white parts were somehow . . . pink? And he smelled distinctly of . . . *garlic?*

"I take it this belongs to you?" said one of the officers.

"Yes! Ohmygosh, thanks so much for bringing him home," I gushed. "He's not . . . I mean, is that red stuff from . . . ?"

"Spaghetti sauce," said the officer, whose name tag read SMITH. "We got a call from Bove's restaurant. Apparently, your mutt likes marinara."

The other officer laughed. "It's good that old Ace here had his identification tag on him," he said. His uniform said CARDELL. "Otherwise, we would've had to take him to the animal shelter."

I shuddered at the thought. Ace had originally come from the Humane Society. What if they had taken him there and someone else had adopted him before I came to rescue him?

"Is Ace under-arrested?" asked Sam, his eyes wide.

I was going to explain what he meant, but Officer Cardell smiled. "Nah," he said. "We just need to talk to your parents. Are they around?"

"Mom is out picking up Ace," said Sam. The officers looked at each other.

"He means our grandpa," I explained.

"Right!" said Sam, brightening considerably now that Ace-the-dog was back and he had the undivided attention of two policemen. "Ace-the-grandpa, not Ace-the-dog!" The officers exchanged another look. I was pretty sure Sam hadn't explained the situation as well as he thought he had.

"Ace isn't in trouble, is he?" I asked.

"Well . . . ," said Officer Cardell.

My mom and Ace came in the door a few minutes after the police officers left.

"TAKE IT TO THE SHOP. THEY'LL TELL YOU. THE BRAKES NEED ADJUSTING," announced Ace. He marched off toward his room without even swiping the crossword puzzle.

"You found Ace?" asked my mom, even though she could see the answer curled up contentedly in my lap. She hung up her coat and turned on the burner under the teakettle.

"Kind of," I said.

"And he's pink because . . ."

"Don't worry, it's not blood!" I said. "What happened was—"

My mom gave Ace a quick pat on the head before cutting me off with "Zelly, sweetie, can it wait? I've got a splitting headache, and I still need to call the insurance company back."

Just then, my dad walked in.

"Hello, monkeys!" he greeted us cheerfully. "Sorry I missed your call, hon," he said to my mom. "Everything okay?"

"Dad! Dad!" yelled Sam, jumping up and down. "The police brought Ace home!"

"The police? What on earth?" said my mom.

"Ace-the-dog or Ace-the-grandpa?" asked my dad in a way that made it clear he was only half kidding.

"It's no big deal," I said quickly. "Ace must have gotten lost, but they found him at Bove's restaurant. Maybe he smelled our scent because we eat there sometimes, so he followed his nose and went looking for us there. Smart, huh? And since he had tags on, they knew where to bring him back, safe and sound." I left out a couple of details, but I figured it was okay since my mom already had a headache. She'd probably appreciate it if I saved the rest for, well, some other time.

"He ate a lady's dinner!" yelled Sam.

So much for saving the rest.

"Which wouldn't have happened if someone hadn't taken him out without permission!" I said, glaring at Sam.

"Wait, what?" asked my dad.

"He let Ace out!" I said, pointing at Sam.

"Not that part. What was that about eating someone's dinner?"

"It's fine. Ace just got into the restaurant through the back door and went into the dining room. He was probably trying to find us. And, well, you know how some people are about dogs."

"The policeman said Ace stood on a table and put his feet on the plates! And he ate a lady's ps'getti and meatballs!" yelled Sam. "So he's gonna have to pay for them!"

"Not him," I corrected. I winced before adding, "But maybe us. The officers said we might have to pay."

"Did they say how much?" asked my dad.

"Seventy dollars, I think," I said quietly. "The bill's on the counter. He might have eaten off a bunch of people's plates."

"They said he liked something called teer-uh-mee-ZOO!" added Sam. "It's not a zoo, though. It's a dessert!"

My dad picked up the bill and put one hand over his eyes. This was not good.

"Interestingly," said my mom in an unhappy voice, "Ace-the-dog was not the only Ace who got into a little hot water today."

"He didn't get into the hot water," corrected Sam. "The ps'getti was already cooked."

My mom had to smile a little at that.

"Oh?" said my dad.

Grateful to Sam for lightening the mood, I looked expectantly at my mom. But instead of continuing, she said, "Zelly, please. Go give Ace a bath. And, Sam, go help her."

I opened my mouth to protest. But then I realized that, one, I wasn't getting a lecture about Ace's bad behavior or a consequence—like *no sleepover*—and, two, if Sam and I left the room, my mom would tell my dad her story about what happened with Ace and the car. Still, she'd be suspicious if I didn't put up a little bit of a fuss, so I gave her one "Do I have to?" to seal the deal. As soon as we were out of the room, I picked up Ace to keep him quiet and told Sam to shush. The three of us froze, listening.

Sure enough, my mom explained about Ace's accident. He had been parking the car when it happened. She said the officers figured he hit the gas instead of the brake, so the car kind of jumped forward and crashed into the car in front of it. Ace, however, insisted that the brakes were broken.

"So it's going to be in the shop for at least a week, probably more," said my mom, "and of course we'll have to cover the damages to the other car too."

"To the tune of?" asked my dad.

My mom mumbled something I couldn't hear, and my dad let out a low whistle.

"Vey iz mir," said my dad, sounding remarkably like Ace. "Never a dull moment. But what matters is, he's okay. He *is* okay, right?"

"I think so. Although, I swear, Nate, he really does seem to be in a fog sometimes. Half the time I talk to him, I don't think he hears a word I say."

"Yeah, and the other half of the time he doesn't listen," said my dad.

My mom laughed softly. "At any rate," she said, "he's home, which is the important thing. They didn't feel the need to keep him for observation. Frankly, I think he was more embarrassed than anything."

Yeah, right, I thought as the spaghetti-slurping scoundrel struggled to wriggle out of my grasp. Ace-the-grandpa is often *embarrassing*. But *embarrassed*? Never.

"What was he doing at the golf course in the first place?" asked my dad.

"You're asking me?" said my mom. Even though I couldn't see her, I could tell she was giving my dad a look.

"Is Grandpa's heart getting attacked again?" whispered Sam, looking scared. He fiddled with the collection of rubber bands he's refused to take off his wrist since Ace went into the hospital last summer.

"Grandpa's fine," I told him.

And I meant it. Ace-the-grandpa was as loud and weird and embarrassing and unstoppable as ever. Ace-the-dog was as rambunctious and wild and untrainable as ever.

What was in critical condition was my sleepover plan.

CHAPTER 8

The next night, Ace appeared at my bedroom door shortly after dinner.

"NU?" he said. "YOU READY FOR CLASS?"

I stared at him, dumbfounded. Ace had been in his room more or less nonstop since Mom had brought him home from his fender bender. Over pizza, she had told me and Sam not to bother Ace, since he was a little "shaky" from the car accident.

"How am I supposed to get to class tonight if Ace doesn't go?" I had asked.

"Well, I suppose I could take you."

"How? Dad has the station wagon and Ace wrecked the other car."

"He didn't wreck it," my mom had said. "But you're right. We're carless at the moment."

"Plus what about Sam?"

My mom had let all her breath out at once. "I'm sorry, sweetie," she said. "It sounds like class isn't in the cards tonight." I had wanted to suggest other ways I could get there, but the tone of her voice told me to drop it. But now it sounded like Ace had worked some magic after I went upstairs.

"We're going?" I asked Ace. It was disorienting to see him acting like his usual impatient self, plus he seemed to be suggesting the exact opposite of what my mom had said earlier. "Did Dad come back or did Mom find us a ride?" I asked.

"NEITHER. BUT I GOT IT ALL FIGURED OUT," said Ace. "GET YOUR COAT."

"Okay, but how—?"

"I TOLD YOU. I GOT IT ALL FIGURED OUT. FOLLOW ME."

Ace-the-dog wagged his whole body with excitement. Clearly, he thought this was a terrific plan!

"Fine," I said, grabbing an extra sweater and my hoodie. Together, we went downstairs.

"Shouldn't we tell Mom?" I asked.

Ace shrugged. "WE'RE OFF TO CLASS," he bellowed.

"What are you talking about?" asked my mom, rushing into the kitchen looking concerned. "You're not supposed to be driving. And besides, Nate has the only working car."

"I MADE A PLAN. WE'RE ALL SET."

"You're getting a ride?"

"NO. WE'RE GOING TO FLAP OUR WINGS AND FLY."

From the look on my mom's face, I could tell she wanted to say something else.

"Please, Mom," I said before she could. "I really don't want to miss class."

My mom looked from Ace to me.

"Mommy!" whined Sam from upstairs. "I can't find Susie." Without her, Sam could not, would not, sleep.

"I'll be up in a minute," called my mom. To Ace, she said, "Okay, fine. Nate can pick you up if you need him to."

"Thanks, Mom," I told her. I ran to catch up with Ace, who was already out the door.

"This is your plan?"

Ace wrapped his scarf tighter around his face and craned his neck, looking up the street.

"DO YOU WANT TO GO TO CLASS, OR DO YOU WANT TO GO TO CLASS?"

"I do, it's just—I thought we were getting a ride," I said.

Either the wind was too strong or Ace was pretending not to hear me. I waited until I caught his eye before yelling my next question: "You're sure the bus runs at night here in Vermont?"

"WE'RE NOT IN THE BOONIES, KID. THIS IS BURLINGTON. THE BIG CITY. OF COURSE THE BUSES RUN AFTER DARK."

"And you're sure they let dogs on the bus here in Vermont?" I asked.

"WHAT IS THIS, TWENTY QUESTIONS?" said Ace.

"No. It's just—how long are we going to have to stand out here? I'm freezing."

"I TOLD YOU TO WEAR A COAT."

"Yeah, but you also told me we were getting a ride. You didn't tell me we were going to stand outside in the cold waiting for the bus. Which isn't coming."

"IT'LL COME," insisted Ace.

"When?" I asked.

"SOON," said Ace. "YOU WANT MY MUFFLER?"

"No," I said, pulling the strings on my hoodie tighter and hugging Ace to my chest. He shivered against me, poor little guy. Just then, the smell of burning leaves hit my nose, making me turn. "What are you doing?"

"WHAT DOES IT LOOK LIKE?"

"Grandpa! Mom said you're not supposed to smoke anymore!"

"WHAT SMOKING?" said Ace, but I could see a stubby brown cigar sticking out from between layers of his scarf. "I'M JUST LIGHTING IT. TO MAKE THE BUS COME."

"That's it," I said. "I'm going back in—"

"AHA!" said Ace. "YOU SEE?"

Sure enough, two blocks away, I could see the bright lights of the bus heading toward us.

"Okay, great, but now what?" I remembered reading a book about Henry Huggins taking his dog Ribsy on a bus in a big cardboard box. But this was real life—how was *that* supposed to work? "They're not going to let us on with a dog."

Ace carefully stubbed out the cigar. He took off the Baxter State and unwrapped his scarf, so I could see that he was smiling. His caterpillar eyebrows started wiggling with excitement. He took one end of the scarf and wrapped it around Ace, who was still in my arms. Then he took Ace from me and turned his back on me.

"GO ON. TIE IT," he instructed. "QUICKLY!" I took the scarf ends, which were sticking out from underneath his armpits and pulled them together, tying a knot, then knotting it again. When he turned around, Ace was pinned to his belly like a fortune cookie fortune taped to the refrigerator. "NOW THE COAT!" barked Ace, so I grabbed it, helping him pull the sleeves back on while nervously looking over my shoulder for the bus.

When Ace got the Baxter State back on and zipped it up around his bulging belly, he looked like a sumo wrestler. Plus, even though he didn't zip it all the way up, I couldn't see Ace, so I worried he was going to suffocate inside.

"What are you doing?! Grandpa, take him out of there!"

"WHAT? HE'S FINE. WHAT COULD HAPPEN?"

"Lots of things! They could kick us off the bus. They could call the police. We could be sent to jail!"

"NONSENSE," said Ace. "BESIDES, AN IDEA THAT IS NOT DANGEROUS IS UNWORTHY OF BEING CALLED AN IDEA. WILDE."

"It's not wild! It's crazy!"

"NOT *WILD*. WILDE. OSCAR WILDE. THE WRITER. HE SAID THAT."

"Oh yeah? Was he wearing a dog when he said it?"

"DOG? WHAT DOG?" said Ace.

Before I could protest anymore, the bus pulled up and the door opened right in front of us. Holding his belly with one hand like he was afraid it might explode, Ace grabbed the handrail and started to waddle up the stairs. I had no choice but to follow. He had my dog.

"AI-YI-YI," grumbled Ace as he carefully maneuvered his way up the bus steps. When he got to the top, he steadied himself on the railing and addressed the bus driver. "A NIGHT LIKE THIS IS NOT FIT FOR MAN OR BEAST."

"Ummm-hmmmm," said the bus driver evenly.

"W. C. FIELDS," Ace informed him.

"Come on, Grandpa," I said.

We walked back and slid into the first available seats, Ace on the left side, sitting sideways and blocking the aisle, and me on the right.

"Did I tell you?" said Ace, whispering for once. "All figured out. Gedaingst?!"

"Of course I remember," I told him. "I just didn't actually think it would work." That was the thing about Ace. Many of his ideas were crazy. But some were so-crazy-they-just-might-work. *Whew*, I thought, *that was a close—*

"You forgetting something?"

I looked up. The voice came from the bus driver, who was staring at us in the rearview mirror. *Oh no*, I thought. *This is the part where we get thrown off the bus. Or thrown in jail. Or worse.*

I looked at Ace. He was leaning very, very far into the aisle, almost like he was about to keel over, still holding his bulging waist with his left hand. He looked very strange, stranger than usual. Just then, I had a scary thought, and my own heart started to pound. *His face was very red. Did that mean something? Was he having another heart attack? What was I going to do?*

"Grandpa?" I said, my voice very small all of a sudden. "Grandpa, are you . . . okay?"

Ace didn't answer. He was reaching behind himself with his right hand while still clutching his "belly" firmly with his left one. *Oh no—Ace!*

I had to do something. So I stood up and started walking quickly to the front of the bus to tell the driver—well, I wasn't sure what. *Excuse me, but my grandpa might be having a heart attack. Oh, and by the way, he has my dog strapped to his belly.*

"ZELDALEH."

I turned, surprised to hear Ace's booming voice, and even more surprised to hear him calling me something other than *kid*. The last time he did, I was pretty sure he was still in the hospital, recovering from his heart attack. But when I turned around, Ace looked normal again. Well, normal for an old man wearing a Budweiser beer hat with earflaps and a dog smuggled under his coat. Normal for Ace. He was waving something triumphantly.

"HERE," said Ace, holding it out to me. I realized why the bus driver was glaring at us . . . and what Ace had been digging out of his back pocket. I ran back to Ace, grabbed his wallet, and practically danced up the aisle to apologize and shove dollars and coins into the fare box. As I sat down again, Ace caught my eye and winked. He unzipped the Baxter State a few inches, enough so I could see Ace snuggled inside, but not enough so Ace could see that he could wiggle his way to freedom.

"SUCH A WORRIER," Ace scolded me after we got off the bus. "YOU COME BY IT HONESTLY."

"What's that supposed to mean?"

"YOU GET IT FROM YOUR MOTHER," said Ace.

The topic of the evening's class turned out to be teaching your dog to heel. Ace, however, seemed to think the topic was attacking the heel of the person who is walking you.

"Ace! Stop it! NO!" I ordered.

"Make it positive, Zelly," coached Mrs. Wright. "If it's not fun for him, he'll lose interest."

I nodded and tried again. "Come on, Ace. Good boy. You can do it."

Ace wagged vigorously and pounced on my shoelaces.

I gave Mrs. Wright a look like *Now what?*

"Wellll," she said, considering Ace, "have you thought about getting those shoes they make that close with Velcro?"

When class ended, I turned to Ace. "Please tell me we're not taking the bus home," I said.

"TOO MUCH EXCITEMENT FOR ONE DAY?"

"Something like that."

"NOT TO WORRY," said Ace.

"Is my dad picking us up?"

"NAH," said Ace. "I CALLED YOUR MOTHER AND TOLD HER WE'D MADE OTHER ARRANGEMENTS."

"Called?" I asked. "What do you mean, called?"

Ace reached into his pocket and pulled out something. It was the basic size and shape of a cell phone, but instead of a keyboard or touch screen, it had a grid of huge buttons with numbers on them. Ace held it out like he had just discovered a new specimen of giant beetle.

"They got *you* a cell phone?" I asked incredulously. Would I have to wait until I was eighty to get one?

Ace shrugged. "I TOLD HER I HAVE NO USE FOR THIS FACACTA THING, BUT SHE INSISTED."

"Zelly, Ace? You ready?" Mrs. Wright had her coat on and was standing next to the door, with Rosie by her side. I had seen Ace talking to her during the bathroom break, but I assumed he was just rattling on about some article he had read. My dad called this "bending your ear," but Mrs. Wright seemed to enjoy having her ear bent. Now she was staring at us expectantly, holding her keys. Rosie looked from Mrs. Wright to Ace-the-dog. Clearly, Rosie had not been consulted when the offer of a ride home was extended.

"*Rufff!*" said Ace-the-dog, fidgeting excitedly. If anyone was not a worrier, it was Ace. He was always thrilled about what might happen next, even if he didn't have the foggiest idea of what it might be. I kind of wished I could be Ace, just for a few minutes, to know what *that* might feel like.

We walked outside to the parking lot and found Mrs. Wright's car. It was a blue Honda, a lot like the one Ace had fender-bended. Come to think of it, Ace had bent a lot of things lately. A fender. People's ears. The truth. Rosie hopped in the backseat first and headed straight for her crate, where she spun once, then lay down on her mat. Mrs. Wright latched the crate, then turned to me.

"I'm sorry, dear, but I don't have an extra crate with me. Can you just hold Ace on your lap?" she suggested.

"IF IT'S ALL THE SAME TO YOU, I'LL SIT UP FRONT," said Ace, climbing into the passenger seat.

Mrs. Wright looked confused. Then she started to laugh. And laugh. "Oh, Ace," she said. "You are a hoot!" Ace laughed too, and Ace-the-dog's tail thumped and thumped. I looked at Rosie. She and I were the only ones who were not amused.

"I'm sorry," said Mrs. Wright to me. "That must happen to you a lot. How on earth did you end up naming your dog after your grandfather?"

"It's a long story," I said.

"THE TRUTH IS, I'M NAMED AFTER HIM," said Ace.

Mrs. Wright started laughing again. "Zelly," she said, "your grandfather is a sketch."

I wanted to tell her that everyone seemed to think my grandpa was a hoot and a sketch. Except me.

"It's very nice of you to be helping Zelly out with her training," added Mrs. Wright. "Does your wife mind you being out every Thursday evening?"

There was a pause.

Then Ace said, "I LOST MY WIFE. EARLIER THIS YEAR."

Lost her? I felt like I was going to throw up. The way he said it, he made Bubbles sound like an old sweater he had left on the bus by mistake. But Mrs. Wright clearly knew what he meant because she said, "Oh!" and then, "Oh, I'm so sorry."

"FEBRUARY," added Ace. "WE WOULD'VE BEEN MARRIED FORTY-SEVEN YEARS IN JUNE."

"Oh, what a loss," said Mrs. Wright. She added, "My husband passed away two years ago." She said it kind of cheerfully, like she had discovered that she and Ace both collected stamps or liked to scuba dive or something.

"MY CONDOLENCES," said Ace.

"Thank you," said Mrs. Wright. "It never really goes away, of course. But, well, there it is."

I couldn't see Ace's face because he had his back to me. But since Mrs. Wright was driving, I could see her eyes in the rearview mirror. I felt very strange. First, because Ace didn't usually talk about Bubbles dying, or about being alone. Second, because Mrs. Wright didn't sound sad. She sounded kind of, well, maybe not happy. But definitely not miserable. Which didn't make any sense. Having someone you loved die felt awful.

When we got to our house, I hopped out of the car first. Actually, Ace-the-dog did—bouncing out the minute I pushed the car door open—but I followed right behind.

"Thanks for the ride!" I yelled before slamming the door. *Yip! Grrr! Yip!* went Rosie, acting tough because Ace-the-dog was no longer in the car.

I started up our front walk before realizing Ace-the-grandpa was still in the car. I paused. Should I wait for him? I kind of had to, since he had the keys, or at least I hoped he did.

A minute passed. Then another. It was really cold. I could've just gone and rung the doorbell to get let in, but I was sort of frozen on the spot, watching Ace and Mrs. Wright. They were talking and laughing, not even noticing that I wasn't there anymore. Finally, the passenger door swung open. Ace steadied himself on the door and the seat and hoisted himself out.

"TILL WE MEET AGAIN," said Ace.

"Eight o'clock Sunday?" said Mrs. Wright.

"IT'S A DATE," said Ace, closing the car door.

Mrs. Wright giggled girlishly. Then she waved and pulled away from our house.

"A *date*?" I said incredulously.

"IT'S NOT A DATE," said Ace.

"You said, 'It's a date,'" I reminded him.

Ace shrugged. "IT'S NOT A DATE," he insisted.

What was wrong with him?! Trying to add my dog obedience teacher to his gaggle of girlfriends? That was too much.

"Grandpa, you can't go out with Mrs. Wright."

"OH? WHY IS THAT?"

"Because . . ." I stopped, not sure what to say. *Because of Bubbles? Because you've already got three girlfriends that we know of? Because what if* Mrs. *Wright finds out you have three other girlfriends and gets mad and takes it out on me and my puppy. Hey, wait, that was it.*

"Because she's Ace's teacher," I announced.

Ace raised an eyebrow at me but said nothing. I took this as a sign that I should continue.

"It would be a—what did you call it? That thing that meant you couldn't judge my proposal?"

"A CONFLICT OF INTEREST?"

"Yes!"

"KID, FOR YOUR INFORMATION . . ."

I stopped paying attention at that point. Ace was in judge mode, bending my ears into pretzels over the legal definition of a "conflict" and how "the doctrine" was "inapplicable in this circumstance." I thought about telling him that I wasn't the one who said it, he was. But arguing with Ace was like playing tennis with Jeremy. He was going to win sooner or later, so sometimes it was easier to just get it over with than to take some feeble swipes at the ball and draw it out.

When he stopped, I slunk off to my room as quickly as I could. Class plus arguing with Ace was a recipe for exhaustion, but for some reason I felt angry instead. All the things I wanted to say but didn't were boiling up inside of me. I clenched my fists, so frustrated I could scream. When did everything get so messed up? I wanted to call someone, tell someone, but who? Allie? Jeremy? Allie thought Ace was funny, and Jeremy thought he was a genius. The only person who would understand what I was feeling—and who knew Ace so well I wouldn't have to explain—was Bubbles.

And Bubbles was gone. She had been for—how long? I unclenched my hands and counted. February to March, April, May, June, July, August, September, October . . .

Eight months. Not even a year.

A year ago, I realized, everything was fine. I still lived in Brooklyn and Bubbles wasn't even sick yet! I had friends there, and I didn't have to worry about getting invited to sleepovers because my friends were just like me—none of us had room in our apartments to have them! And my Brooklyn friends were like me in other ways too. Some were Jewish. Some had frizzy hair. Some even had frizzier hair than me! And being the new kid was never a big deal because practically everyone in Brooklyn is from somewhere else.

Of course, I didn't have a dog when I lived in Brooklyn. But having a dog wasn't anywhere near as easy as I'd thought it would be, even with all the "practice" Ace made me get with my stupid "practice dog," O.J. My gaze fell on O.J., who now sat on my bookshelf, grinning his goofy hand-drawn grin as always. When I no longer needed a practice dog, I had considered putting O.J. out with the recycling—after all, he was just an old orange juice jug. But for some reason, I couldn't do it. So I gave him a job holding all my loose change. He wasn't such a great substitute for a dog, but as a bank, he was okay. I hadn't put any money in him or given him any thought for weeks, but the way I was feeling now, everything about him set me off.

Put it this way: I didn't quite see red. But when I saw O.J., I definitely saw *orange*. Everything was Ace's fault. Ace and his dumb ideas! I jumped up, grabbed O.J., and threw him across the room. He hit the wall so hard it knocked his cap off. Seeing his chance to join the attack, my puppy pounced from my bed, grabbed O.J. by the handle, and shook him vigorously from side to side.

Shucka-shucka-shucka . . . Coins rattled loudly, causing Ace to drop O.J. and stare at the jug in alarm.

Ace's reaction surprised me and momentarily took my mind off my anger. Curious, I picked up O.J. and gave him a big shake. *RAH-KAH-RAH-KAH-RAK* rattled the coins, echoing inside O.J.

"*Hrnnnnnn!*" whimpered Ace miserably, sinking to the floor. With his little shoulders hunched up, he lay there, whimpering and shaking.

"Acey, honey, I'm sorry. You okay?" I asked. It was weird—he'd never reacted like this to anything. Ace relaxed, then shook it off and chomped his squeaky banana like nothing had happened. Just to check, I picked up O.J. and gave him another, smaller shake.

"*Hrrrnnnnn!*" whined Ace again, dropping once more.

Very weird, I thought. Even O.J. seemed surprised.

Well, that got his attention, his grinning face seemed to say.

"You stay out of it," I told O.J., even though I was pretty sure that talking to a plastic jug was a sign that I was completely losing it. Just the same, it made me feel a little better. And a little sorry, so I got up a few minutes later and retrieved him. No matter how much it drove me nuts sometimes to remember everything Ace-the-grandpa had put me through,

O.J. still felt weirdly real to me. So I couldn't just leave him there on the floor, where Ace-the-dog would inevitably launch another, more successful attack.

Knowing my puppy, it was only a matter of time.

"How's Ace doing with his classes?" asked Jeremy the next morning on the way to school.

"Not so good," I admitted. "He doesn't seem to be getting the hang of it."

"Have you tried adaptive behavior therapy?" suggested Jeremy.

"Adoptive what?"

"*Adaptive* behavior therapy. It's something my dad studies." Jeremy found his dad's work as a psychologist endlessly fascinating. "In order to get someone to change behavior, you expose him over time to those who can model the desired behavior until he catches on."

"Like introducing Ace to some normal grandpas?"

"Actually, I was talking about Ace-the-dog."

"Yeah, I know," I said. "But 'over time'? How much time? There's less than two months until the test. Plus your dad studies people, not dogs."

"Yeah, but same diff. Think about it. You know dogs that behave better than Ace, right?"

"Pretty much every dog I know," I admitted.

"Well, so, remember when you were walking all those other dogs before you got Ace? What if you borrowed one of them to show Ace what he's supposed to do when you give him a command?"

"I guess," I said dubiously. My dog-walking business, The Zelly Treatment, had closed down when school started up. But all of the customers were my neighbors, so it would be easy enough to borrow a dog. "But there's no way hanging out with a well-behaved dog is going to magically turn him into one."

"What have you got to lose?" asked Jeremy.

Jeremy had a point, I realized. And if any dog could demonstrate how a well-trained dog should behave, it was Bridget. She was calm, focused, and able to do all the obedience basics, even with her limited vision and hearing. Plus Ace adored Bridget.

But that was also the problem: Ace loved Bridget. So when I brought Bridget over to our house to practice, Ace grabbed his squeaky banana, then wiggled around, teasing her, and barking. When I got Bridget to demonstrate a down-stay, Ace took a flying leap with a mighty *rrrowfff!* and jumped on top of her like it was a game.

"Ace! No! Get off!"

The next day, I borrowed Bridget again. I invited Jeremy to come over so I could demonstrate the weaknesses of his theory.

"You try," I suggested.

"Bridget," Jeremy said firmly. "Sit."

"She can't really hear you," I reminded him.

"Oh, right," said Jeremy.

"Wait, though, check this out." I did a hand signal, and Bridget immediately sat.

“I thought she couldn’t see, either.”

“She can’t! I mean, okay, she can probably see something. But not much—look how cloudy her eyes are. Now it’s your turn, Ace. Sit!”

Instead, Ace jumped up and pounced, landing with his front paws out, shoulders lowered, and rump in the air, in his best ready-to-play position. Bridget slid from her sit into a down by default.

“You see what I’m dealing with?” I said to Jeremy.

“Let me try again,” said Jeremy. “Hey, Ace,” he continued, his voice high with excitement. “Here, boy, look!” Jeremy raised a tennis ball high above his head. “You want this? Huh, huh, you want this?”

Oh boy, did Ace want that. His head jerked up and down, following the ball as Jeremy moved it. His eyes locked in a staring match with the tennis ball.

Jeremy gave the ball a good bounce on the floor to make his point. Clearly, this was too much for Ace, who barked excitedly, then threw himself at the ball and Jeremy all at once—*whomp!*—knocking Jeremy down and sending the ball bouncing off over his shoulder. Ace bounded over Jeremy, snatched his prize triumphantly, and trotted back to a spot juuuuust out of reach of Jeremy. He narrowly missed sitting on Jeremy’s glasses, which had flown off when he fell. Jeremy groped around on the floor and located them.

At which point, Ace saw the only thing more tempting to him than a neon-yellow ball: a face to lick. He dropped the ball and pounced on Jeremy.

"Ace, no!" said Jeremy, shielding his nose with his arm. "Zelly, hey, get him off me!"

"Ace, NO! SIT!" I said, grabbing him sharply by the collar and lowering my voice threateningly.

At which point Ace looked up at me.

And smiled as if to say *Oh, hi there!*

"Admit it. He's totally hopeless," I said.

"I think you were onto something with the way you made your voice all deep. He looked like maybe he wanted to sit."

"GREAT," I growled, as loud and low as possible.

"We're making progress. It's just going to take a lot more Bridget," said Jeremy stubbornly.

"How'd it go?" asked Mrs. Stanley when I went to return Bridget.

"Not so great," I admitted. "I mean, Bridgie was perfect. Ace, on the other hand . . ."

"Don't give up, honey," said Mrs. Stanley. "Rome wasn't built in a day, right? Plus Ace is still just a puppy. Aren't you, sweetie?" She bent down to ruffle his ears, but Ace took the opportunity to try to eat her sports watch.

"Ace! Come on!" I pried him off Mrs. Stanley's wrist.

"Hang on a second, Zelly. Let me get some money," said Mrs. Stanley.

"Oh, that's okay," I said. I had walked Bridget for money over the summer, but it didn't feel right for her to pay me when Bridget was helping me train Ace.

"Zelly." Mrs. Stanley put her hands on her hips, mock-scolding. "You earned it. Put it aside for a rainy day, all right?"

"Okay, fine."

"Quarters okay?"

"Sure." I accepted a handful from her. When I got home, I popped the cap off O.J. and dumped them inside.

O.J. smiled back at me. *Yay, money! You're that much closer to paying off Ace's restaurant tab*, he seemed to say.

"Thanks," I said, replacing his cap and patting him on the "head."

"Good dog, O.J.," I told him.

CHAPTER 9

"What about a spaghetti dinner?" I suggested.

"Nah," said Allie. "But I like the food idea. How about bacon and eggs!"

"Bacon and eggs?" I said dubiously, digging the toe of my boot into the dirt and shoving my mittens deeper into my pockets, even though it made it harder to balance on my swing. Since Halloween was two days away, Allie and I were spending our recess huddled on the swings, keeping an eye out for errant wall balls while brainstorming costume ideas.

"What? I like bacon and eggs! If you don't want to be bacon, you could be the eggs."

"Allie, duh," I said. "You know I'm not kosher. Plus, even if I was, it's not like I'd be eating you."

Allie laughed. "Well, then, why not?" she asked.

"*Smelly Fried Egg?*" I said, even though I hated repeating what Nicky Benoit used to call me.

"Come on, no one remembers that," protested Allie.

"They will if they see me dressed like a fried egg!"

"Fine," said Allie. "But I still think it's a good idea. Hey, maybe Jenny can be eggs? You can be something else."

"Okay," I said, twisting my swing around. The metal chain got tighter and tighter. Trying not to sound too disappointed, I asked, "Like what?"

"Hmmm," said Allie, considering this. "I know! You could be O.J."

I stopped twisting and gave her a look. Allie's forgetfulness could be irritating sometimes. "O.J.?" I said flatly.

"What?" said Allie. And then, "Oh, right."

Even Allie couldn't claim that no one would remember that particular episode.

As I unspun myself, I racked my brain trying to come up with something good to be. The year before, I had been the Statue of Liberty, using a green bedsheet, a foam headdress, and a flashlight torch. I guessed I could do it again, especially since moving to Vermont meant no one had seen me wear it already. Not that it mattered to some people—Sam had been Batman for about five years straight, although this year it was looking like Luke Skywalker would win out. Frankly, I kept hoping he'd be something else, since he wore his Luke Skywalker bathrobe so often it was almost as much of a schmatte as Susie-the-whale. If I had worn something like that, my parents would definitely have told me to change. But with

Sam, they were impressed that his dedication to all things Skywalker was not limited by, say, cleanliness.

The next morning I came down to breakfast to find my dad scrambling eggs. This was unusual on a school morning, but I wasn't about to complain. It was also unusual that all five of us were at the kitchen table at once. Ace and Sam were playing crazy eights while my mom sipped coffee and read the *Burlington Free Press*.

"CLUBS!" said Ace, laying down the eight of clubs, which turned out to be his last card. He grinned. "BETTER LUCK NEXT TIME."

"Next time? Know what I want to play next?" Sam asked. Before Ace or anyone else could answer, Sam took all the cards and threw them up in the air at once. "Fifty-two pickup!" he yelled, bursting into giggles.

"Sam!" said my mom sharply. She picked the three of hearts out of her coffee cup and handed it, dripping, to him with a dark look.

"Aw, man!" said Sam, sliding off his chair to gather up the cards.

At that moment, Halloween costume inspiration struck. I'm not sure why. Maybe because the cards flying made me think of those wisecracking Ace-card-men. Maybe because of my mom's coffee mug.

"Hey, Mom, do we still have that old laundry basket?" I asked.

"The yellow one with the broken handle? I think so. If memory serves, it's in the basement housing your grandfather's golf ball collection. Why?"

"Oh, no reason."

When I got home from school, I went down to the basement and relocated Ace's golf balls. I called my dad and asked him to pick up some poster board. When he got home, he helped me wrap it around the laundry basket and glue it in place to make the sides and the handle.

"I love it," said my mom when we let her see. "Wait, can I make a suggestion?"

"Um, sure."

My mom ran upstairs and came down with a big tan scarf and a wicker basket that turned out to be filled with sewing stuff.

"I didn't know you could sew," I said nervously as she wrapped the scarf around my shoulders and pinned it in place.

"I can't do anything fancy," she admitted. "But I can get by. My mom taught me."

"Were these hers?" I asked.

"Umm-hmm," said my mom, because she was holding five pins between her lips. It gave me a warm feeling, and not just because the scarf was cozy. In a small way, it was like Bubbles was there with us. I thought about Bubbles' painting kit, which had been given to me. I didn't even like to open it, much less use the paints and brushes, because they smelled like her and made me sad. But the sewing things felt different somehow.

After a few minutes, my mom stood back. "There," she said, "good to the last drop." I shuffled over to check out my costume in the mirror. I gotta say, it looked pretty good. I could hardly wait to show Allie. Eggs, bacon . . . and me as a mug of coffee. If we could convince Megan to be toast, we'd have the best group costume ever!

One huge bonus about moving to Vermont was that I could finally go trick-or-treating with just my friends, which my parents never would've let me do in Brooklyn. They almost said no, but Allie helped convince them by promising that her big sister, Julia, would be with us. But since they were still feeling a little nervous, my dad stopped me at the door and handed me something.

"You got me a cell phone?!"

"Ha-ha, very funny."

"So, why are you giving me Ace's cell phone?"

"I'm not. I'm loaning it to you for the night."

"Yeah, that's okay," I said. I could just picture the looks on my friends' faces when I pulled out the big bug phone with the number buttons.

"Take the phone," instructed my mom. "It'll be good practice for when you're old enough to get one of your own."

"Fine," I said, thinking, *Sure, when I'm so old I don't even see the point of having one anymore.* I turned around carefully. "But you'll have to put it in my pocket for me. I can't reach."

My mom slid her hand down the back of my cup. I leaned to one side to help her gain access. Watching us, my dad started whistling "I'm a Little Teapot."

"Dad!" I said.

"Sorry, sorry!"

"Okay, here's the deal," said Julia when her friends showed up to meet her. "You have a watch, right? So just meet us in front of the Mahoneys' house at nine-fifteen. Don't be late or else. Got it?" Allie and I nodded. "Be good little girls," called Julia over her shoulder. Her friends laughed as they headed off together.

"You are so lucky," I told Allie, who rolled her eyes in response. But before she could start up about Julia, Jenny came running up wearing a store-bought egg costume.

"Hey! You guys!" Jenny put one hand up, out of breath. As soon as she pulled it together, though, she gushed, "Zelly, you look great!"

"Ahem!" said Allie, posing.

"Bacon!" Jenny grabbed Allie and pretended to chomp her. "Om nom nom nom!"

"Cut it out," yelled Allie, swatting Jenny with her treat bag. "Seriously, stop it!" she yelled. "You're going to rip it!" But she was laughing too.

It was the best Halloween ever. We picked up Megan, whose toast costume was kind of lame but at least she agreed to do it. She was wearing brown clothes with a big brown triangle of construction paper stapled to the front of her shirt and a small yellow square of construction paper stapled to that to be the butter. Everybody told Megan she looked awesome, which made me wonder if they were just saying my coffee cup looked cute because that's what you do. I decided not to care because the whole point of a group costume is having something that goes together. Which we totally did.

"Hey, it's the Breakfast Club!" someone said. At almost

every house, people called us cute or clever. Some of them even took our picture. We got tons of candy.

Then, all of a sudden, Jenny yelled, "Hey, I know. Let's go to the Cunninghams'!"

"Ooh, yeah!" yelled Megan and Allie, dashing off with her.

"Wait, where?" I said, scurrying as fast as I could in my cup, trying to keep up with them. "Hey, Allie, wait!"

The scarf was coming undone. Plus the cup's base was narrow, so I couldn't separate my knees enough to get up much speed. Allie slowed down and gave me the scoop. Every year, a family named Cunningham transformed their home into a haunted house. It was awesome and scary and they always had the best candy.

"Full-size!" she said. "Not fun-size."

"No way!" I said, trying to sound thrilled. I didn't know how to tell her that I had never been in an actual scary haunted house, and I was pretty sure I didn't want to. "Except I, uh . . ."

"Yeah?"

"I just remembered I have to go home and walk Ace," I told her.

"Aw, really? Can't you just do it after?"

I shook my head. Now that I had invented an excuse, it felt like a real obligation. "You could come with me and we could meet up with those guys after," I suggested.

Allie didn't answer right away. At the sound of laughter, she turned in the direction where Jenny and Megan had run. "I . . . guess . . . ," she said slowly.

"You guys! Come ON!" I heard Jenny yell from a distance.

"Gahhhhhhhh!"

I jumped at the sound, and out of nowhere, Jeremy appeared, brandishing a sword. Or at least, Jeremy's head, arms, and legs appeared. The rest of him was hidden inside a huge box, which had been painted to look like a cornflakes box . . . with red paint splashed all over it.

"Is Seth with you?" asked Allie, who claimed she no longer had a crush on Jeremy's older brother but wasn't convincing anyone. She looked around hopefully.

"Yeah, right," said Jeremy, rolling his eyes. "He ditched me ages ago. Plus he's not even dressed up. I was with Scott and Jason and everyone, but now I can't find them."

"What are you supposed to be?" asked Allie.

"Guess!" said Jeremy, posing with his sword up. Allie and I stared at him.

"Cap'n Crunch?" tried Allie.

Jeremy sighed and shook his head. "Zelly?" he said.

I studied him for a minute. "Oh, wait, I know. You're a cereal killer! That's awesome."

"Thank you!" said Jeremy, attempting to take a bow. "Oof! It's really hard to bend in this thing."

"Join the club," I said.

"What are you?" asked Jeremy, tilting his head to one side and considering my costume. "Some sort of pun about getting mugged?"

"No, she's a cup of coffee," said Allie.

"And you're . . . bacon?"

"Yes," said Allie impatiently. "Zelly, are you coming?"

"Remember? I can't. I have to go take care of Ace first," I said.

"Want me to go with you?" asked Jeremy.

"Yeah, sure," I told him. "How about if I meet you there after?" I asked Allie.

"Okay, fine. But hurry up! It's on Overlake. You can't miss it." And with that, she took off after Jenny and Megan.

"So," said Jeremy, "did you get a lot of candy?"

"Tons," I said. We compared hauls, did a couple of quick trades, and set out for my house. As we walked, he fished a pack of gummy body parts out of his bag.

"Brain?" he offered.

I took one.

"Just so you know, that haunted house is pretty lame," said Jeremy. "You'll see."

"Not if I can help it," I said. "Why do you think I said I had to walk Ace?"

"Zelly!" Jeremy stopped walking. "Now we *have* to go."

"What? No! Haunted houses freak me out."

"Yeah, but I told you, this one is a joke. Come on, if you face your fears, you won't be afraid anymore. It's called aversion therapy."

"Arrgggh!" I groaned. "Don't go getting all shrinky on me."

"Just trust me, okay? Plus they have the most awesome candy—"

"Yeah, yeah, I know. Full-size, not fun-size," I said. Fine, we'd go to the Cunninghams'.

It wasn't hard to tell which house it was. There were tons

of kids all over the lawn, plus lots of spooky decorations, including crime scene tape around their fence. I spotted Allie, Jenny, and Megan right away, talking with a bunch of other girls. I decided to sneak up and surprise them. Jeremy stayed at the fence while I hid behind a bush. I heard Allie's voice first.

"That sounds awesome!" she said. I was about to jump out when I heard her say, "You're so lucky that you get to invite everyone." I froze, waiting to hear more.

"Well, not *everyone*." I peeked out and saw that the voice belonged to Hailey Larson, who was in my science class. She was dressed like a cheerleader, but her face was painted white like a zombie or something. "My stepmom said no more than ten plus me. But my dad said we can stay up all night! It's next Thursday, and there's no school on Friday."

"You know Zelly Fried, right?" asked Allie.

"Zelly? Yeah, I know her," said Hailey.

"Are you going to invite her?"

"I don't know," said Hailey. From her voice, it sounded like she was wrinkling up her nose. "Why?"

"Well, see, I had this sleepover last summer," said Allie. "But Zelly had to leave because her grandpa got really sick. He almost *died*."

"No way," said Hailey.

"Uh-huh, and she hasn't been to one since then," said Allie dramatically.

"Wow," said Hailey. "But I kind of already decided who I'm going to invite. And I don't really know her that well."

"You should invite her," said Allie. "She's really . . ." I

waited to hear how Allie would describe me. The word she came up with was *funny*.

"Yeah, okay, maybe," said Hailey. She didn't sound very convinced.

I stood there, unable to move. I felt so confused. On the one hand, it sounded like a sleepover invitation might be coming my way! But what was up with Allie? I didn't like hearing her talking about me that way.

Was she doing it to be nice?

Or because she felt sorry for me?

And how exactly was I *funny*? Funny like . . . Ace?

I backed out of the bushes and ran off to find Jeremy before anyone could see me.

"Jeremy, let's get out of here!" I said.

"You can do this, Zelly! Face your fears."

"It's not that! Uh, the line is too long," I said. "Anyway, Ace needs a walk. Come on!"

I grabbed him by the arm and pulled him with me.

"Take it easy!" protested Jeremy. "This thing is really hard to move in."

Racewalking awkwardly, we made it down the block, around the corner, and all the way to my house. I needed to clear my head and figure this out. Was what just happened good or bad? Both? Or neither? My mind was reeling, and I felt like I was going to be sick.

"Hold on," I told Jeremy when we got to my front door. "Let me grab Ace. I'll be right back."

"Actually, can I use your bathroom?" asked Jeremy.

"Sure," I said, ringing the doorbell. No response, not even the barking that usually ensued immediately. Could Ace have taken Ace for a walk?

I fished around under the doormat in the dark and came up with our spare key. Jeremy followed me in the door.

The minute we stepped into the house . . .

"Whoa—"

"What the—?"

. . . an overpowering and unmistakable smell assaulted us.

Dog poop.

The kitchen floor was covered in what looked like brown spray paint and confetti. Wandering through the first floor, stepping as carefully as I could, I saw that the mudroom, the living room, and—*oh no*—Ace's bedroom had all received the same treatment. And worst of all, Ace-the-dog was nowhere to be found.

"Ace? Ace!" I called, my voice sounding nasal—I was plugging my nose—and increasingly frantic. Jeremy and I spread out and searched the house.

"Zelly! He's here."

I ran to the upstairs bathroom. There, lying on the bath mat, panting pathetically, was Ace.

"Ace! Oh no!" I grabbed the phone and called my mom on her cell phone. *Please pick up, please pick up*, I thought, hoping she wasn't so busy navigating the dark streets with Sam and my dad that she wouldn't hear it ring. Finally, I heard her voice. "Come home quick," I begged, and luckily she did. She took one look at Ace and called the vet, then handed me the phone, then took it back to write down a number and call the emergency vet line. I bundled Ace up in a towel, wincing as my mom explained the situation over the phone. "I don't know. Maybe thirty or forty pieces in all?" she said, a worried look on her face. "Uh-huh, milk chocolate. Maybe in the last hour or so?"

"I can't believe this," I said to my mom in the car. "How did Ace get into the candy?" I had a momentary pang of guilt. My dad had wanted to hand out Halloween stickers and toothbrushes. I was the one who talked him out of it.

"I don't know, sweetie," said my mom. But I could tell from the look on her face that we were both thinking the same thing. Ace-the-grandpa had been the only one home. He'd probably answered the door, then left the candy where Ace-the-dog could get it and went out. His note, rubber-banded to the pepper mill on our kitchen table, simply said:

OFF TO SEE A FRIEND.
BACK LATER!
ACE

"Poor Ace," said my mom.

"Poor *Ace*?!" I said bitterly. "He's the one who's responsible for this!"

"I meant the dog."

"Oh," I said. I kissed my puppy and stroked his velvety ears.

"Let's not be too hard on your grandpa. You know he loves Ace too."

I snorted at this suggestion. Mr. My-Bedroom-Is-Off-Limits? Mr. Rolled-Up-*New-York-Times-Magazine*? Mr. Leave-the-Chocolate-Where-the-Dog-Can-Reach-It? Right!

Ace whimpered in my lap. I petted his head, wishing I could do something, anything, to make him okay. *Just make Ace better,* I silently prayed.

I remembered making that same request once before, only when I did, it was for Ace-the-grandpa, so I added, *Ace-the-dog, that is. And I'm sorry for only asking for stuff when there's a problem. Please don't get mad at me for that. Please just make Ace better, okay?*

I thought about what Jeremy had said about me not going to Hebrew school. Maybe I should check that out after all. Not so much for getting a bat mitzvah. But so that I had someone to turn to when things got rough. And so that when I needed to call in a favor, the response wouldn't be *Zelly who?*

CHAPTER 10

The vet's office was so brightly lit and so busy you would've thought it was the middle of the day, not late at night. Since Ace was in critical condition, they offered to put us in an examining room right away. I took it as a good sign that Ace did his usual routine of pulling determinedly toward the front door before I scooped him up and carried him, whining pitifully, to the assigned room. A vet tech arrived and checked his temperature and vital signs before whisking him off to the back.

Letting go of Ace was the hardest part. I had this spooky feeling that I would look back on this moment as the last time I saw him. My mom was still at the front desk filling out some paperwork, and I felt so scared and alone. I thought about Bubbles and I wished she was there to tell me everything would be okay. Even more, I wished she had been there with Ace-the-grandpa to keep him from leaving the chocolate where my puppy could get it.

Since the doctor came in before my mom did, I tried my best to answer questions about Ace and the events leading up to his emergency room visit. What had he eaten? Chocolate, lots of it. Milk only, no dark. When? Probably within the last hour or two. Had he been vomiting or having diarrhea or "loose stools"? Yes, yes, and yes. Having seizures? That hadn't occurred to me, but I hadn't seen him have one, so I guessed that was good.

We ended up being there until midnight, at which point they brought a very sleepy Ace out to the waiting room, where I had fallen asleep in a chair. He looked tiny, maybe from all the throwing up, but the vet assured me he'd be fine in a few days. We went over some ground rules about not leaving potentially poisonous items where Ace could "access" them, and I got a handout listing all sorts of things that could make him sick.

I guess the one good thing about the whole experience was it completely took my mind off what had happened at the Cunninghams' haunted house.

Allie was waiting for me on our corner the next morning. She greeted me with:

"Zelly! What happened to you last night? You missed everything!"

I opened my mouth to tell her the crazy story of my awful night with Ace.

Then I closed it.

I wanted to tell her everything, including the part about hearing her telling Hailey about me. But I wasn't sure I wanted to hear her pretend she didn't know what I was talking about. Or try to defend what she did with some lame excuse. I wasn't sure I wanted to hear her make something up. Or tell me the truth, whatever it might be.

Instead of waiting for an answer, Allie just kept right on talking. "The haunted house was awesome! And then Scott and some of the boys knew this other house, and they had all these bowls of candy out front, but then there was this hand thing in one of the bowls, and all of a sudden it moved! And Jenny ran to get away, but she wasn't watching where she was going . . ."

Allie kept talking and talking, not even noticing that I hadn't said a single thing. *Maybe we'd make it all the way to school,* I realized, *without me uttering a single word. Was she always like this? How had I never noticed?*

". . . and the whole scene was just so bizarre!" Allie concluded her story. "Seriously, you should have been there. You would have loved it!"

Great, I thought. *Now I'm funny and bizarre too.*

"I tried calling you when I got home," said Allie.

"Yeah, sure," I grumbled.

Allie looked confused. "What's wrong? Why are you acting so weird?" she said.

"I'm not acting," I said, quickening my pace so she had to sprint to keep up. "That's just how I am." *Funny, bizarre, and weird.*

At school, everyone was talking about Halloween, of course, and swapping candy whenever my English teacher, Mrs. Clements, turned her back to write on the board. When lunchtime rolled around, I got my milk and scanned the room, not sure I wanted to sit at my usual table. But the only other option was with the boys, so I made my way across the room.

"Hey, Zelly," said Jenny. She was sitting next to Megan and across from Allie.

I forced a smile and sat down. Not in the spot next to Allie that she always saved for me, even though seat-saving was not, technically speaking, allowed. Instead, I sat down on the other side of Jenny. "Hey," I said back.

If Jenny thought it was strange that I was avoiding my regular seat, she didn't say so. Instead, she immediately turned her back on me to examine something Megan had in her hand. I leaned over and saw that it was a little piece of paper. At first I thought it was a candy wrapper, but when Jenny saw me peeking, she quickly slipped it into her pocket.

"What's that?" I asked.

"Oh, nothing. It's just, you know, for Hailey's thing."

"What thing?" I asked innocently.

"It's nothing, just a sleepover," said Jenny.

"I'm sure she'll invite you," added Allie brightly.

Yeah, but only because you told her to, I thought.

"Hey, what happened to you last night anyway?" asked Megan with a grin. "You just, like, disappeared."

"Yeah," said Jenny. "One minute you were there, and then, *poof*!"

"I had to go walk Ace," I said.

"With anyone special?" asked Megan, batting her eyelashes at me. Jenny and Megan looked at each other, then burst out laughing. *Of course*. Allie must have told them that Jeremy went with me. Jenny and Megan remained convinced that Jeremy was secretly my boyfriend, even though I had told them a million times he was just a friend.

"Yeah, ha-ha," I said. "For your information, my dog ate tons of chocolate. He had to be rushed to the emergency room. He could have died."

I ran out of the lunchroom and spent the rest of lunch hiding in a stall in the girls' bathroom, waiting for the bell to ring and trying not to cry. I couldn't believe Allie! *Why did my so-called best friend think I was so funny-weird-bizarre-pathetic I needed someone to beg for invitations for me?* She had made everything worse! I wished we had never moved here. If I were back in Brooklyn, Ace wouldn't live with us, I would have real friends who saw me for me, and stupid sleepovers would be a nonissue.

That night, I went up to my room right after dinner. I was exhausted from the night before, so I lay down on my bed with a book and got good and lost in it. So lost, in fact, that when my mom came in to tell me I had a phone call, she startled me awake.

"It's Allie," she said, holding it out to me.

I shook my head. "Tell her I can't come to the phone," I mouthed.

"O-kay," she said. She got back on the line, and I heard her walk out saying, "Allie, hon? She's already in bed. Yes, Ace gave us a scare last night, but he's going to be fine. . . ."

Meanwhile, Ace-the-grandpa had replaced my mom in the doorway. He was wearing the Baxter State, plus his muffler and his ice-fishing hat. In his hand was a leash. Attached to the end of it was Ace-the-dog.

"YOU READY FOR CLASS?" he asked.

"No," I told him.

"OH? WHY NOT?"

"I changed my mind. I don't want a sleepover."

"WHAT ABOUT THE DOGGELAH? WHAT ABOUT WHAT HE WANTS?"

"It doesn't matter, Grandpa. Ace can go by himself for all I care!" I snapped. "I'm not going."

I lay down, turned to face the wall, and braced myself for a lecture on how quitters never win and winners never quit, or something like that. Instead, I heard my door close. Exhausted, I shut my eyes.

A little later, I sat bolt upright in bed. My room was dark. I felt around in my covers. "Ace?" I said.

No Ace.

I ran downstairs. "Ace!" I called. I knocked, then opened the door to Grandpa's room.

No Ace. Neither Ace.

Then it hit me:

Ace had gone to class. With Ace. And without me.

But why? I told him I had given up on getting a sleepover. The answer came to me a split second later: Mrs. Wright. Ace loved attention, and Mrs. Wright heaped it on him. "It's a date," he had said when she dropped us off, and she had giggled.

Oh no, I thought, shuddering. *Don't tell me he's up to four girlfriends . . . that we know of.*

When I woke up the next morning, Ace-the-dog was snuggled up in my bed next to me, sleeping soundly. Clearly, it didn't bother him at all that he had snuck off to class without me. My mom came in a couple of times to make sure I was getting up, and I convinced her to drive me on account of the fact that what the weatherman called a "wintry mix" was coming down outside.

"Should we offer Allie a lift?" she asked.

"Her dad drives her and Julia when it rains," I told her. I felt a little guilty for not checking, even though this was usually the case. I thought about the possibility of her standing on the corner waiting for me and I felt bad, but not bad enough to call her.

I had a lousy day at school. Mr. Tortoni gave us a pop quiz on probabilities, but I couldn't focus on it. All I could think of was the probabilities of my life: *If one girl is allowed to invite ten friends but ends up inviting eleven girls, one of which is not really a friend, what is the probability that the eleventh girl will ever actually receive another sleepover invite? If one dog refuses to stay in one place longer than five seconds ninety percent of the time, what is the probability that he will flunk out of obedience class for the second time?* Then, in English class, I couldn't find my pen, so Mrs. Clements did what she usually did: took one of my shoes as "collateral" on getting her pen back. I wiggled my toes as I wrote, feeling angrier and angrier. At Mrs. Clements, at Allie, and especially at Ace-the-grandpa. I went to the nurse during lunch. I lay there with a wet paper towel on my forehead and watched icy raindrops chase each other down the window until I heard the bell ending after-lunch recess.

When I got home from school, I practically tripped over one of Sam's creations. It was a tower made of paper cups, drinking straws, LEGOs, and a deck of cards. I called, "Ace!" as always, but he didn't come. "Mom?" I tried.

"I'm in the basement," she called back.

"Sam!" I yelled next.

Sam came running, lightsaber in hand. "Halt, who goes there?" he said, facing off with me.

"Where is he?" I demanded.

"Where is who?"

"Ace, Sam! Where's Ace?"

"Oh!" said Sam. "They're in the living room."

"They?" I asked, but the answer was immediately obvious. Ace and Ace. Ace-the-grandpa was holding a little metal ball in his right hand and was periodically clicking it. In his left hand was a half-eaten hot dog. Ace-the-dog was staring at it, licking his chops.

"What are you doing?" I asked.

"SIT," he ordered, ignoring me. Ace-the-dog sat down. I heard a click and saw Ace toss Ace a little piece of hot dog. Ace inhaled it in one gulp.

"SUCH A FRESSER," Ace told my puppy.

"What's that sound?"

"WHAT, THIS?" said Ace. He clicked it at me—*click! click!*—a few more times before handing it over so I could inspect it. It was a small, familiar-looking round brass gizmo, sort of like an old-fashioned pocket watch. When I clicked it myself, I realized where I'd seen and heard it before.

"Isn't that what Bubbles used to use to count knitting rows?"

"YUP," said Ace. "IT'S FOR KNITTING AND SITTING."

"I don't think this is funny," I said.

"SO DON'T LAUGH. HERE—YOU TRY."

Ace handed me the leash, lowered himself onto the couch, and stared at me.

"I wasn't at class," I said pointedly.

Ace hoisted himself up again. "THIS ISN'T FROM CLASS. WE'RE TRYING SOMETHING NEW," he said, sounding pleased with himself. "AND YOU'RE WELCOME."

"You're welcome?" I said in frustration. "For what?"

Ace frowned. "I TOOK HIM TO CLASS. I DID YOU A FAVOR."

I was beginning to see orange again. I knew if my dad was here, he'd be trying to defuse the situation with a nice plate of celery, cream cheese, and raisins right about now ("Ants on a log, anyone?"). But my dad wasn't here.

"That's not a favor!" I shouted. "A favor is when you ask for something! I didn't ask you to do that."

"Zelly, I'm using the Force now," said Sam, pointing his lightsaber at me. "Stop yelling."

"Plus what about Halloween?! Did it ever occur to you that Ace could have died from all that chocolate?" I continued, ignoring Sam. "No—all you cared about was going on your date! All you ever care about is yourself!"

"FOR YOUR INFORMATION, KID—"

"I'm gonna die!!!"

Ace and I stopped yelling and turned to look at Sam. He was no longer pointing the lightsaber at us. He was shaking and his eyes were huge.

"SAM, WHAT ARE YOU TALKING ABOUT?"

"Zelly said so! I ate all my Milky Ways even though Mom said to just have one," he confessed.

"Not you," I said. "Ace."

Sam's bottom lip started to quiver, and his hand flew to his rubber band bracelets. "*Gwampa's* going to die?" he whispered.

"SURE, EVENTUALLY," said Ace.

"Grandpa!" I said sharply. "Look, Sam, I was talking about Ace-the-dog. Dogs can die from chocolate, not people. But he's fine. Grandpa's fine too."

"Fow weal?"

I nodded. Sam looked to Ace, and he nodded too. Sam let out a long breath, shuddered, then said, "Can I watch TV?"

"YES," Ace and I said together, even though we both knew the answer was supposed to be *Check with Mom*. For once, I was actually glad to see Ace disregarding a rule. With Sam gone, Ace turned to me.

"LOOK, KID—" Ace started to say, but I wasn't in a mood to have my ear bent. So I pulled Ace out of the living room by his leash and dragged him right into . . .

Auughh!

—the crazy house of cards that Sam had built.

It was not as dramatic as throwing them up in the air, but the result was the same. All the cards—and cups and LEGOs and drinking straws—went flying, landing all over the floor in every direction.

Great, I thought. *Fifty-two pickup. Story of my life*.

"I'm sorry," said Ace.

"I don't want to— What?" It was disorienting to hear Ace's voice at a fraction of its usual volume.

Ace sat down carefully on the ottoman. "I just wanted to help you out," he said feebly.

"Yeah, well, thanks. But don't," I said. "Usually it makes things worse."

Ace started to use his cane to sort of sweep the mess in the same direction. It wasn't a very good tool for the job, so most of the cards stayed put.

"Hold on. I've got it," I told him. I didn't like to see him looking so defeated and, well, old. Cranky, feisty, loud-mouthed Ace drove me crazy, but dejected Ace was actually worse. I sat down on the floor and used my hands to gather the playing cards.

"I had no idea about the chocolate business," he continued. "We never had dogs." He pulled out his handkerchief and wiped his brow. "Look, kid, I can't tell you how sorry I am. Me and my mishegoss. If I hadn't been in such a hurry to go out, this never would have happened."

"It's okay," I said. For someone who rarely apologized, Ace was surprisingly good at it.

"I get antsy being in the house by myself," Ace admitted. "Too quiet."

"Me too," I told him.

"Also, I shouldn't have taken him to class," added Ace.

"He didn't, by any chance, do a better job without me there?" I asked hopefully.

"NOPE," he bellowed, his usual decibel level returning, along with the color to his cheeks. "WORSE."

I knew that shouldn't have made me feel better. But for some strange reason, it did.

CHAPTER 11

As Allie "predicted," I did indeed receive an invitation to Hailey's sleepover. The fabulous Thursday-night-before-no-school-Friday sleepover that everyone who was anyone was going to.

Except me. Because I declined it. Reluctantly.

Which made Allie grumble the entire way to school when I told her. "Give me one good reason why you're not going," she said.

Nope! I thought. *And I wouldn't hold my breath if I were you.* In the days since Halloween, I had successfully squirreled my anger at Allie away to the back of my mental nut-storage, thus enabling me to spend my lunch periods in the cafeteria instead of the girls' room. Once or twice, I had been tempted to tell her. But the more time passed, the more it felt like that would make too big a deal out of it. I pictured Allie telling Jenny and Megan—or, worse, telling all the girls at Hailey's house—about it. *You know Zelly Fried? She is such a drama queen! First, she spied on me, then she got mad over nothing and wouldn't even tell me what was wrong!*

And I had almost convinced myself that maybe it *was* nothing. I mean, what was so bad about Allie asking Hailey to invite me anyway? *I should just feel grateful to be invited*, I told myself, *not mad about why*.

But it didn't feel like nothing. It felt like something had changed with me and Allie. Or maybe it was always this way, but I was so busy assuming everything was fine or not paying attention that I didn't see what was obvious to everyone else: Allie had lots of friends, not just me. She was the center of our lunch table, her class, and the sixth-grade social universe altogether. Me? I was the popular girl's *funny* friend. And if that wasn't bad enough, she felt sorry for me. She practically said so.

"I have to take Ace to dog obedience class," I told her. "I missed last week. So I'm kind of behind already. Plus my grandpa will be mad if I blow it off."

"Zelly! Your grandpa won't even notice! Isn't he kind of, you know . . ." Allie looked like she was trying to think of a polite way to say something that wasn't so nice. She went with "Busy? With all his girlfriends and everything?"

"He'll notice," I told her.

But I'll admit I was tempted. What if Ace didn't mind if I missed class? After all, he hadn't lectured me when I didn't go the week before. It would be pretty silly to turn down Hailey's sleepover without even asking him, wouldn't it? It couldn't hurt to ask.

So that evening, I knocked on his door.

"Ace?"

"Ruff!" At my feet, Ace-the-dog barked once. Maybe because he heard his name and was expecting a treat. Maybe because he was announcing our presence in puppy language.

"WHA?"

"Hi, Grandpa. Can I ask you a question?"

"YOU JUST DID." I smiled weakly. "ALL RIGHT, ALL RIGHT," he said. "ASK ME ANYTHING."

"Hypothetically speaking," I said, using one of Ace's favorite techniques to try and get on his good side, "do you think it would be disastrous if a person missed dog obedience class for a very good reason?"

"THAT WOULD DEPEND," said Ace, snapping into judge mode, "ON THE CIRCUMSTANCES. WOULD THIS PERSON HAVE ALREADY MISSED ONE CLASS, HYPOTHETICALLY SPEAKING?"

"It's possible," I admitted.

"WELL, THEN, I WOULD SAY THAT WHILE IT MIGHT NOT BE DISASTROUS, IT COULD HAVE SERIOUS IMPLICATIONS ON THAT PERSON'S LIKELIHOOD OF PASSING THE FINAL TEST."

"Oh."

"MOREOVER, THERE IS A SOCIAL COMPACT INHERENT IN PARTICIPATION IN A COLLABORATIVE TRAINING ENDEAVOR. HOWEVER, WHEN WEIGH-

ING THE IMPLICATIONS OF ONE'S ACTIONS ON OTHER PARTICIPANTS, ONE MUST REMEMBER—"

"All right, all right, I'll go," I said, caving under the weight of the lecture. "I just thought maybe you'd appreciate having the night off."

"THIS ISN'T ABOUT ME, KID. THIS IS YOUR CALL."

"But isn't that what you just said?" I asked.

"NOPE. I SAID WE MUST BELIEVE IN FREE WILL—WE HAVE NO CHOICE. ISAAC BASHEVIS SINGER."

I tilted my head to one side. Ace-the-dog copied me. "So, you're telling me to go to class."

"NOPE."

"Okay, well, what would you say if I said I'm not going to class?"

"I WOULD SAY I HOPE YOU HAVE A GOOD REASON."

"I do," I said. "I got invited to a sleepover."

"WHICH IS WHAT YOU WANTED IN THE FIRST PLACE. RIGHT? YOUR PROPOSAL AND THE SEVENTEEN GIRLS STAYING OVERNIGHT?"

"Not seventeen," I said. "But yes, I just—"

"YOU DON'T WANT TO LET ME DOWN."

"Actually, no. I mean, I don't, but that's not it." I hesitated, and then I confessed, "I wasn't really invited. I mean, I was, but only because Allie told the girl to. So now I don't really feel like I should go."

"OKAY, SO DON'T GO."

"But I really want to go—"

"SO GO."

"Just not like this."

"LOOK, KID, YOU'RE MAKING ME DIZZY. GO, DON'T GO. JUST LET ME KNOW WHAT YOU DECIDE."

I looked at him. "That's just it. How do I decide? They both feel wrong."

Ace shrugged. "THEY MIGHT BOTH BE WRONG."

"Or they might both be right, right?" I asked.

"RIGHT," said Ace. "AND YOU KNOW WHAT THREE RIGHTS MAKE?"

I shook my head.

"A LEFT," said Ace.

I tilted my head like Ace-the-dog, more confused than when I started.

"JUST THINK ABOUT IT," said Ace.

"The three-rights-make-a-left part?"

"ALL OF IT."

Two wrongs? Three rights? Too much! I just wanted to go to the sleepover! And Ace had said it was my decision, even though I wasn't sure I believed him. So I decided to go. The hoot Allie let out when I called to ask for a ride—a much better reaction than the noncommittal grunt I got from Ace—confirmed that I had definitely made the right decision. My mom gave me a funny look when I mentioned the last-minute change in plans, but when I told her Ace was okay with it and she didn't have to drive me anywhere, that seemed to satisfy her. Even though I had already packed

Ace a treat bag for class, I left it on the counter and went upstairs to pack something even better: a sleepover bag. I put in my pajamas and my toothbrush and toothpaste, plus my sleeping bag and a throw pillow shaped like a heart. I grabbed my glasses case and was about to pick a book from my bookcase when—

Whatcha doing?

I looked at O.J., sitting on top of my bookcase, staring at me with that goofy grin of his.

"What does it look like?" I told him. "I'm packing for a sleepover."

Oh? What happened to earning your own sleepover?

"It's okay. I can miss class one night."

But this'll be the second time. Do you really think Ace is going to pass if you don't go to class?

"Look," I told O.J. "Even if I work my hardest, Ace still might not pass. And then I won't get to have a sleepover. And then I won't get any sleepover invitations. This way, at least I get one."

Yeah, but do you want to go to a sleepover you weren't really invited to?

Ouch, I thought. For a plastic pup, O.J. had quite a bite. "Leave me alone," I said. "You don't know what you're talking about. You're not even real."

O.J. continued to stare at me, grinning cheerfully. *Besides, wasn't the point to prove you could do this? To your parents, and Ace, and everyone? Do you really want to give up so easy?*

"No," I said. Because I wasn't giving up. Or was I?

You worked really hard to prove you were responsible enough to get a dog. And now you have to work even harder to prove you can stick to what you set out to do.

"I don't want to prove anything. I just want to be like everybody else."

But you're not like everybody else. You're weird, and everyone knows it. Just look at yourself! You're talking to a plastic jug.

Get a grip, Zelly, I told myself. Just the same, I turned O.J. to face the wall so he'd stop making me feel so guilty. I selected one of my favorite books, *The Book of Three*, from the shelf and noticed that a chunk was missing from the cover and it had telltale tooth marks all over it.

I groaned. "Ace!" I yelled.

At the sound of his name, Ace came running. He had something red and round in his mouth. I grabbed Ace by the collar and reached down to take away the tomato he was—

"Ace! No! That's not for— ACE!"

In my hand was Bubbles' pincushion, slightly damp and full of sharp pins and needles. Ace beamed up at me as if he expected me to toss it for him to fetch. Inspecting it, I was relieved to see that Ace had probably just swiped it. But as I held it, it dawned on me that this wasn't just about winning a sleepover. If Ace didn't learn how to behave, and soon, he might have bigger problems than making a mess or embarrassing my parents in front of company. He could seriously hurt himself, or run off again and— I didn't want to think about it.

Setting the pincushion on the top of my bookshelf, next

to O.J., I hooked a finger under Ace's collar. I led him out to the hall and grabbed the upstairs phone with my free hand. I dialed Allie's number again, and when she answered, I explained that I wouldn't be coming after all.

"Arrggghhhh! Zelly! What is your problem?"

"I'm sorry," I said. "I just need to see this whole training thing through. I can't let O.J. down."

"What?"

"I can't let Ace down."

"You said O.J."

"No, I didn't," I said.

"Yeah, well, whatever," said Allie. "Look, I've got to go."

And she hung up the phone.

I almost called her right back. *Just kidding!* I wanted to say. *Zelly, you crack me up*, Allie would say. *You're so funny that way!*

Funny. How was I funny? Funny like Ace? I didn't want to know the answer.

Slowly, I put the phone down and released Ace. "Grandpa," I yelled, heading down the stairs, my puppy nipping at my heels.

"You just missed him," said my mom, who was playing cards at the kitchen table with Sam.

"No, seriously?" I said.

"Margie picked him up in her punch-buggy-no-punch-back," announced Sam. "You gotta see it, Zelly. It's yellow and there's stickers all over it! It's the coolest car ever! Except maybe a hovercraft, only that's not exactly—"

"Sam, we get it." I ran to the window and looked left and right—no such car in sight. "Did he say when he'd be back, Mom?"

"I don't know, sweetie. Why?"

"I have to get to class."

"But I thought you were going to a sleepover?" My mom gave me a confused look. "Didn't you say Allie's mom was picking you up?"

"Yeah, well, it's a long story but I'm not. Okay?"

Confusion shifted to concern. For a fleeting second I wondered if Ace had grumbled to her on his way out the door. But instead of commenting on my change of heart, she just said, "Well, try calling him."

I dialed his number from the downstairs phone, but when I did, I heard a tinny version of "If I Were a Rich Man" from *Fiddler on the Roof* coming from the mudroom.

"Mom, he forgot his phone again!"

"Okay, relax. We'll figure out something."

"Thanks for giving me a ride, Mrs. Stanley." I slid into the backseat of her car, buckled my seat belt, and pulled Ace into my lap. Bridget, buckled into a harness next to me, turned her murky gaze in our direction. I petted the two dogs at once, one squirmy, one sedate, both sweet.

"Sure, Zelly, happy to help. How's Ace doing with his classes?" she asked.

"Uh, he's doing okay," I said.

"Good for him!" said Mrs. Stanley. "Bridget was such a disaster at that age. Weren't you, Bridgie?"

Bridget's tail twitched repeatedly. It could have been a muscle spasm, but it really looked like a wag. She had been mostly deaf and almost blind the whole time I'd known her, but some days she could fool you into thinking she wasn't missing a thing.

Mrs. Stanley shook her head ruefully. "Such a little troublemaker. Chewing on everything. Howling at all hours. We had to pull up all the rugs. And she ate all our socks!"

"Ace too! He tried to eat a pincushion today. And did you hear he ate a bowl of candy on Halloween and had to go to the emergency room?"

"Oh no. Poor baby! Bridgie did that twice, once on Halloween, once on Easter."

"Bridgie? Really?" It seemed crazy that mellow old Bridget could have once been as bad as—or worse than—Ace.

"Mmm-hmmm," said Mrs. Stanley. "Such a mischiefmaker. Even after we taught her what was what, Bob had to retrain her several times."

"Retrain her?" I asked. This hadn't occurred to me. I kind of assumed that training a dog was sort of like riding a bicycle: once you had the basics down, you were all set.

"Sure," said Mrs. Stanley. "You know, to keep her up on her skills, keep her from picking up bad habits. Of course, she's slipped a lot lately, but that's to be expected," added Mrs. Stanley. "Even with her joint supplements and her other pills, she's not very comfortable sitting or standing, poor old girl.

And it's got to be confusing for her not knowing where she is half the time."

"I'm sorry," I said, talking to both Mrs. Stanley and Bridget at once. For some reason, I started thinking about Ace-the-grandpa. He wasn't very comfortable sitting or standing, either, and yet he was willing to sit in an old folding chair for an hour at class every week.

We stopped at a light and I noticed an old woman in a bright pink coat standing on the corner next to a bus sign. I smiled, remembering Ace waddling onto the bus with Ace smuggled under the Baxter State. I felt bad for causing Ace-the-grandpa to miss class after he had been so determined to get me—and Ace-the-dog—there. I petted both dogs, glad to be sandwiched between them.

When Mrs. Stanley dropped me off, I went inside and found Mrs. Wright walking Rosie around the orange cones in the otherwise empty training area. I'd never been this early for class before. Mrs. Wright came to a halt when she saw me, and Rosie immediately sat.

"Zelly! Good to see you. We missed you last week, didn't we, Rosie?"

Rosie, hearing her name, stared up at Mrs. Wright, wagging her tail expectantly. Mrs. Wright tossed her a piece of cheese. "Where's your grandpa?" she asked.

"He, uh, couldn't make it tonight." I felt bad that it probably seemed like he was blowing the class off, when in fact I was the reason he wasn't there.

"Is everything okay?" she asked, her face concerned.

"Oh yeah, he's great. He's just, um, not here. Is it okay that I don't have a grown-up with me?"

"Of course," said Mrs. Wright.

"Also, can I ask you a favor?" I asked.

Right before class started, I used Ace's cell phone to call Mrs. Stanley. "I'm all set," I told her. "My teacher can give me a ride home."

It was a long evening. The focus was on the command "stay." I couldn't help finding my thoughts drifting to Hailey's sleepover. I wondered what they were doing. I couldn't help wishing that instead of having to "stay" here, I could "go" there. So did Ace, apparently. He refused to stay in one place, sitting, standing, or lying down.

"Ace, stay!" I tried. Again and again and again.

"Maybe he has ADHD," suggested the man with Lady, the Great Dane. *Not helpful*, I thought, frustrated. His dog wasn't so perfect. Lady could do "stay" for hours, but he practically had to sit on her to get her to lie down.

"Why don't you stay-ay-ay just a little bit longer?" sang Mrs. Wright to Ace. To demonstrate his inability to do just that, Ace stood up on his hind legs and danced to the tune, clowning for a treat. *Hopeless!* I thought, not for the first time.

Finally, thankfully, class ended. Mrs. Wright and I walked our dogs to her car.

"Do you want to sit up front?" asked Mrs. Wright. "Tonight I've got an extra crate Ace can use."

"Oh, that's okay," I told her. "I can just sit in the back and keep him on my lap."

Mrs. Wright started the car, and I reminded her of the way to my house.

"Your grandpa did a great job last week," said Mrs. Wright. "Ace is really coming along."

"Right!" I said sarcastically.

"He is! He's a smart boy, and he'll get there, just you wait and see."

"Thanks," I said.

"He's quite a character, your grandfather," she added.

"Yup," I said.

"My husband was too. Your grandpa reminds me of him. Same kind of strong . . . personality."

I could see her smiling dreamily in the rearview mirror. *Oh no*, I realized. She had the same goofy look Allie reserved for her number one crush, Seth. Mrs. Wright was falling in love with Ace! While Ace was just being a flirt. He was already dating three other people, one of whom he was out with right now!

I felt really sorry for Mrs. Wright. She was a nice lady. Which is maybe why I blurted out, "Mrs. Wright, do you have a boyfriend?"

"Nope. Do you?"

"N-n-n-o," I stammered, feeling my face get hot and immediately wishing I had kept my mouth shut.

Mrs. Wright smiled and said, "I'm just teasing, dear. Why do you ask?"

"To tell you not to go out with my grandpa."

"Oh!" said Mrs. Wright with surprise. "Really? Why not?"

"Well, see, he had a heart attack."

"Oh my goodness!" said Mrs. Wright. "Why didn't you say something? Is he okay?"

"He's fine," I told her quickly. "It wasn't, like, yesterday. It was over the summer. I'm only mentioning it because since then he's been acting, um, crazier than usual. He means well. He's not a bad person. But lately he's started doing all this stuff he's not supposed to do."

"Like what?"

"Everything. Eating things he's not supposed to eat, smoking cigars, getting into a fender bender, going out dancing with lots of different ladies . . ."

"And that's upsetting to you?" asked Mrs. Wright.

"Uh-huh," I admitted.

"I see," said Mrs. Wright. And then, "*Lots* of different ladies?"

I nodded meekly.

"How many is lots?"

"*Three,*" I whispered. "That we know of."

"Oh my," said Mrs. Wright.

"You can't tell him I told you!" I said.

To my surprise, Mrs. Wright laughed out loud.

"Zelly, hon," she said, "let me tell you a story about a lady I know. She married her college sweetheart, the love of her life. He was smart and clever, a real charmer. He had a gorgeous singing voice and a full head of hair. And I can assure you, that is a tough combination to come by! But the thing is, this man, he passed away."

"I'm sorry," I said, because that's what people said when they heard about Bubbles. It's what you're supposed to say, even if you didn't know the person.

"Thank you, sweetie," she said. "Anyway, this lady, she was alone for a while. But she realized it wasn't so great, being alone. So when she met a new friend or two who would take her out for a coffee, maybe even take her dancing, she began to see that there was something nice in that. Even if they weren't the love of her life. Does that make sense?"

"Not really," I admitted.

"Your grandpa's grieving," said Mrs. Wright. "So if going dancing distracts him from his pain, then maybe he needs to go dancing right now."

"Ace isn't grieving," I informed her, almost starting to laugh at the idea. "He never gets sad or cries or anything. I mean, I don't cry so much about my grandma anymore, but—" And then I realized I was crying. Mrs. Wright pulled the car over and found me a Kleenex in her purse. I blew my nose and rubbed my eyes. Ace-the-dog happily slurped up my salty tears. Rosie paced nervously in her crate.

"I'm sorry," I said.

"Don't be," said Mrs. Wright. "Two things, kiddo," she said to me. "One, your grandma was special. No one will ever take her place. In your heart or your grandpa's. Two, we all grieve in our own time and our own way. Trust me, I know."

I nodded, mostly by way of saying thanks. I was still pretty sure she was wrong about Ace grieving. But even so, Mrs. Wright made me feel a little better.

"*Yapp!*" added Rosie from her crate.

And then Mrs. Wright turned around in her seat again, pulled her car back into traffic, and drove me the rest of the way home.

CHAPTER 12

"How was the party?" I asked Allie on the phone the next day.

"Actually, not so great," she said.

"Oh?" I asked, perking up.

"I mean, it was okay," said Allie.

"Did you get to stay up all night?"

"Almost," said Allie. "That was fun, but Hailey was being super-bossy. She got mad at her stepmom over nothing and locked herself in the bathroom and wouldn't come out. Total drama queen."

"Wow," I said, making mental notes for if I ever got to have a sleepover. *Don't be bossy, no drama.*

"And get this: she said to bring movies, but then she didn't want to watch anything anyone brought. I brought *Bringing Up Baby*, and she was like, 'Ugh, that's not even in color!'"

"Seriously?" I asked, secretly thrilled. I had given Allie a DVD of that movie after my dad made us both watch it—I think Allie and I said, "Ugh, it's not even in color!" at the time, but I wasn't about to remind her of that—and we'd decided it was our favorite movie of all time.

"Yeah," said Allie. "It was pretty lame. Your sleepover is going to be soooo much better."

I couldn't help smiling. "It totally is," I agreed.

There was just one little problem.

One little, furry, floppy-eared, brown and white problem.

Fine, I told myself. *You can do this. You still have a month. You just need to work that much harder.* I made myself a list of all the things I could do:

1. More practicing with Bridget
2. More practicing, period
3. No more skipping class, no matter what

On Sunday evening, after Ace broke his stay for at least the fifty seven millionth time and attacked a spider plant, I added one more thing:

4. Professional help

I picked up the phone and dialed. A little while later, the doorbell rang.

"Dr. Pavlov, at your service," said Jeremy, bowing formally, one hand on his kipa.

"Thank goodness you're here, Doctor. There's not a moment to lose!" I replied, letting him in.

I had pretty much begged him to come over and help me solve Ace's behavioral problems. "You know how I usually tell you not to get all shrinky?" I had asked him. "Well, for this, bring it on—the shrinkier the better. We need to figure out why Ace won't do what he's supposed to do in order to make him stop."

"You mean start?" asked Jeremy.

"Stop, start, whatever. Make him pass the test!"

Jeremy must have been thrilled about the chance to go all mad scientist on my dog, because when he showed up on my doorstep, he was rubbing his hands excitedly.

"Where's the patient?" he asked.

"Destroying something, I'm sure," I told him. "Come on, let's get to work."

"What I wouldn't give for you to have that attitude about math tests," called my mom from the mudroom. She emerged fully immersed in outerwear, from the soles of her tall Sorel boots to the pom-pom atop her knitted hat.

"Can I have a sleepover if I ace a math test?" I asked.

"Nice try," said my mom. "Nate, you ready to go?"

"Almost," said my dad, carrying his boots in and sitting down in front of the woodstove. "Thanks again, Zellybean, for agreeing to stay here and keep an eye on the Sam-wich."

"Yeah, it was a tough decision," I said sarcastically. "You know how I hate to miss a good square dance."

"Laugh if you want, but I hear it's hip to be square," said my dad, lacing up his boots.

"I seriously doubt that," I said.

"It's true. Just ask Ace," insisted my mom. "He has been going every Sunday night for months. Apparently, your dog-training teacher goes dancing there too."

I froze, remembering how I had warned Mrs. Wright about Ace's shenanigans. Wait, what had she said to Ace that evening she drove us both home? *Eight o'clock Sunday? It's a date*, Ace had replied.

Oh no. She was talking about square dancing.

What an idiot I was! She already knew he went dancing. In fact, she was one of his many dance partners. What's more, she was okay with it. *Everyone grieves in their own time and their own way*. Was Mrs. Wright wiser than I realized? Was Mrs. Wright, well, *right*?

After my parents put Sam to bed and headed out, Jeremy and I got to work. We pushed all the living room furniture around to make space for a sort of makeshift practice ring.

"Okay, what's the plan?" asked Jeremy.

"Well, in class we practice commands with the dogs and give them treats if they do them right. As they get better, you're supposed to give them fewer treats."

"Food is a good motivator?" asked Jeremy, pulling out a little notebook and jotting down this important detail.

I rolled my eyes. "Jeremy, duh? Have you spent any time with dogs? Ace tried to eat a pincushion because it looked like a tomato. Even Bridgie will work for food, and I don't think she can smell anymore."

"Okay, so what else motivates him?"

I thought for a second. "Praise, I guess. On the rare

occasion when he's actually being good. Hey, Ace, stop! No! Drop it!"

Ace froze, one of my gloves sticking out of his mouth. His tail wagging slightly—*Who, me?*—he tried to wiggle his way out of the room without actually dropping it. I lunged at him, grabbing his collar and reclaiming the now-slimy glove.

"Reprimand . . . not . . . a . . . deterrent," observed Jeremy, scribbling furiously.

"Nope!" I said cheerfully. "Nothing makes him stop. Not spraying him with water, or yelling, or taking stuff away, or anything else. I mean, we don't hit him, obviously, but none of the stuff that's supposed to work does. He's completely clueless."

"You mean fearless."

Fearless? Ace? I suddenly remembered something. "Actually, no. There *is* one thing that stops him in his tracks," I said. "Wait here. You've got to see this." I ran up to my room and came back down with . . .

"O.J.!" said Jeremy. "I didn't know you still had him."

Meanwhile, Ace stood frozen, his eyes on the jug in my hands. "Watch this," I told Jeremy. "Sorry," I apologized to Ace in advance. And then I held up O.J. and gave him a good shake.

RAH-KAH-RAH-KAH-RAK went the coins inside.

"*Hrnnnnnn!*" whimpered Ace miserably, immediately flattening himself on the floor at the first sound of The Awful Noise.

"Whoa!" said Jeremy. I held O.J. silent for a moment while

Ace slowly got up, shook himself, and walked over to the couch, eyeing O.J. suspiciously.

"I know," I agreed. "Isn't that weird?"

"What's in there?"

I took the cap off O.J., poured some of the coins out into my hand, and showed him. "Just money," I said.

"So, O.J. is a tzedakah jug now?"

"A what?"

"It's where you keep loose change, you know, for charity. At Hebrew school, they hand out these blue metal boxes you can use, but a jug is kind of cool."

Ace wandered over, still timid but clearly not wanting to miss out in case it was food. I showed Ace the handful of coins too. "See?" I said.

"Don't be afraid," said Jeremy. "It's just change. Hey, that's funny. He's *afraid of change*. Get it?"

"You can see why I can't use O.J. to train him," I added. "It's too mean."

"Yeah," agreed Jeremy. "Well, okay, do you have something that makes a sound but doesn't make so much noise?"

"Like what?"

"I don't know. How about something that makes a clicking noise."

I stared at him. "Have you been talking to my grandpa?"

"No, why?"

"Because he's got this knitting thing that used to be my grandma's, and he's started clicking it at Ace."

"Wow! He's clicker-training him?"

"It's a real thing? I thought he made it up. I mean, he also thought it would be a good idea to train Ace using Yiddish."

"Yeah, it's real. Lots of professional animal trainers use some variety of clicker training. The dolphin trainers at the New England Aquarium use it too."

"Okay, well, I wish he'd explained that. Hang on."

I ran to Ace's room and got the clicker off his nightstand.

"Ace, sit!" I said. *Click*, *click*.

Ace cocked his head to one side and stared at me. *Click*, *click*, I tried again. Ace walked over and tried to take the clicker out of my hand. With his mouth.

"No, Ace!" I said, holding it out of reach. Ace barked, then put his paws up on my legs to try to reach it.

"It's impressive," said Jeremy. "In my entire professional career, I've never seen anyone so determined to do the wrong thing."

"Just like my grandpa," I said. "Did I mention that on top of everything else, my dog-training teacher's in love with him?"

"So, that makes four girlfriends that we know of?" asked Jeremy.

"I really hope not." I sighed. "So, tell it to me straight, Doc. Is he a hopeless case?" I thought about the man with the Great Dane shaking his head and asking if Ace had ADHD.

"I don't think so," said Jeremy. "Just because Ace isn't perfect, you shouldn't throw everything out the window."

"I'm not throwing anything out the window. I'm just trying to get Ace to stop being so . . . Ace!"

"Wait, which Ace are you talking about?" asked Jeremy.

"Who's on first?" I replied, smiling.

"I don't know," said Jeremy.

"Third base!" we both said together. He knows the routine almost as well as Sam.

"Jinx!" I yelled. Jeremy started waving his arms wildly almost immediately. There's nothing Jeremy hates as much as not being allowed to talk.

CHAPTER 13

"Three weeks to go, Acey, see?" I circled the date on the calendar and showed him. Ace barked and jumped up, trying to see if the pen was a stick. "No, Acey, come on, you know better than that! You're doing great, and with a little more practice, you're going to ace your test. Get it? *Ace* your test!"

Ace barked again. *That's my name!*

"Mazel tov," I told him. "Let's see you do some of the trickier stuff." He was a lot shakier on the stuff that came after week one: heeling on a loose lead, doing "down" the first time he was told to instead of the fifth, and, of course, not popping up when he was told to "stay." I could tell he knew that he wasn't released until I said "okay," but he didn't seem able to resist the temptation to squirm in place, then wiggle, then run around. Sometimes he'd scratch himself or shake as an excuse to break his "stay," and then he'd give me a look like *What? I was just shaking!*

By far, holding his "stay" when I left the room was the hardest part for him. No matter how many times I told him otherwise, and no matter how many times I came back *just like I said I would*, he seemed convinced that if he couldn't see me, I was gone forever.

"It's called object permanence," Jeremy had explained to me. "It's a developmental stage. Before babies develop object permanence, they think that things that are hidden don't exist anymore. I guess it's the same with puppies. Ace thinks when he can't see you, you've disappeared forever."

"Weird!" I said. But it actually made sense. No wonder Ace was so excited every day when I came home from school! "So how am I supposed to convince him that I'll always, always, always come back?"

"Maybe you can't," said Jeremy. "I mean, think about it. Ace came from the Humane Society, right?"

"Yeah. Why?"

"Well, clearly he had a mother once, and littermates, but he doesn't know where they went. It's possible he even lived with another family before your family and one day they disappeared too."

"I never thought of that," I said.

Jeremy shrugged. "Or maybe it's one of those cognitive things and he'll just develop it at some point. I don't know. My dad studies people, not dogs."

I had to admit that something about what Jeremy said made me less frustrated with Ace and more sympathetic toward him. The poor little guy had lost his mom, after all. Luckily, he had me. And he had another maternal figure in his life: Bridget. Since she was such a good role model, I found myself "borrowing" her more and more as the test got closer and closer.

"Wanna go get Bridgie for a walk?" I asked Ace. At the sound of the word *Bridgie*, Ace's ears perked up, and when I said *walk*, he went flying down the hall to grab his leash off the hook himself.

"Hold on, hold on," I laughed, pulling my boots on and grabbing a hat, mittens, and a down vest. When I got to my feet and claimed one end of the leash, Ace gave a yank and practically dragged me out the door. Outside, he squatted immediately, then tried to kangaroo his way across our lawn before getting frustrated by the snowdrift.

"Gotcha!" I said, scooping him up and stealing a kiss before depositing Ace on the skinny path of cleared sidewalk my parents had managed to keep exposed. Ace bounded along, breaking into a run when he got to the Stanleys' front walk. Mr. Stanley always puts down salt and Ace always forgets, then starts hopping and whining and trying to sit down and lick his feet. To avoid this, I grabbed Ace again and carried him up the Stanleys' front steps.

I rang the doorbell. *Bing-bong-bang-bing*. I heard it echo inside, like always. But, unlike always, I didn't hear Mrs. Stanley yell "Coming!" or the sound of Bridget following Mrs. Stanley down the hall, howling *arooooooo* because she couldn't hear herself anymore.

I tried knocking, which got Ace barking. Then I rang again.

"I guess they're not home," I told Ace, peering through the window beside the front door, even though the Stanleys have lace curtains that make it pretty impossible to see anything inside except dark shapes. Like the light brown and white lump on the long rug that runs along the side of their staircase. Which looked like a pillow or a pile of laundry or—*a dog?*

I bent down and flipped open the mail slot, then stuck a finger in and opened the other side. Ace made a funny whining noise.

"Oh my—Bridgie? Bridgie!"

Ace was trying to lick my face because it was down at his level, and now that I was saying "Bridgie," he was getting more and more excited, wagging like crazy. It was like he thought we were playing some dog version of hide-and-seek and any moment now Bridgie was going to jump out of hiding, like Bubbles once did when she came for a surprise visit when I was really little.

Except Bridget wasn't hiding. Or jumping. She was lying there.

Don't panic! I thought. *She's probably just asleep*. "Bridgie!" I yelled through the mail slot, even though I knew her hearing was lousy. "Bridget, wake up."

Hrrnnnnn. Ace started to whine. The game wasn't fun anymore. Where was his walking buddy? Where was Bridget?

"Come on," I told him. I got up and ran down the stairs, forgetting all about the salt and everything as I dashed back to the sidewalk and retraced our steps to our front door.

"Mom?! Mom!" I yelled, feeling the tears of fear and desperation coming even though I had only been gone five minutes. I knew she was there.

My mom came running. "Zelly, what on earth?"

"It's Bridget. She's not moving and I think she might be hurt or something."

"What? Where?"

"At her house. I went to see if she could take a walk with Ace, but no one's home and she's just lying there."

"Okay, hang on."

My mom grabbed her coat, then followed me back over to the Stanleys', Ace racing at our heels. Mom rang the bell just like we had and put her nose up to the glass window beside the door. She cupped one hand to her face to get a better view through the lace. I showed her the view through the mail slot.

"Oh dear," she said.

"Maybe she's just asleep," I told her.

"Maybe," she said, but it didn't sound like maybe. I burst into tears as my mom took out her cell phone. She dialed, and after a pause I heard her say, "Maureen? Hi, it's Lynn Fried." Even though you don't have to say that on a cell phone, Mom always does.

I grabbed Ace and ran down the walk so I wouldn't have to hear what came next. I just wanted to go home, to go back, to make it so I had never taken Ace out, never seen what I saw, make it so it didn't even happen. When I got home, I found that our door was locked, so I sat on our front step and pulled

Ace into my lap. I buried my face in his fur and cried, hugging him so tightly I thought he'd squirm away or whine, but he didn't. Maybe he needed that too. After all, Bridget was his friend as much as she was mine.

"Zell?" I looked up to see my mom standing there. "Sweetie, let's go inside. You'll freeze out here."

"She's not . . . ?"

My mom nodded. "I'm so sorry, Zelly."

"No!" I yelled, surprised at how angry I felt. "You're wrong. You don't know what you're talking about!"

"I wish I was," said my mom quietly. "I used my spare key to let myself in and check on her, sweetie. I'm so sorry." Ace cocked his head to one side, trying to figure out what was going on. My mom took out her keys and opened the door.

"I want to be alone," I announced when we got inside. I stomped past Ace, who was doing the crossword puzzle at the kitchen table, and went to go dump my boots and outerwear. From the mudroom, I heard Ace ask Mom, "WHAT'S WITH GRETA GARBO?"

"Dad," said my mom sharply.

"WHA?"

"It's the Stanleys' dog," my mom whispered, but loud enough to make sure Ace could hear. "Bridget? She passed away."

"SHE RAN AWAY?"

"No, Dad. *Passed* away."

"HIT BY A CAR?"

"No."

"BUS? YOUR MOTHER USED TO LOSE A CAT A WEEK TO THE—"

"No, Dad, not the bus. Sha!"

I didn't want to hear any more, either. I stomped back through the kitchen and up to my room, Ace scampering to keep up with me.

I heard the phone ring a couple of times, but I didn't even think of running to get it like I would otherwise. I didn't want to talk to anyone, not even Allie or Jeremy. Ace hopped up on my bed, circled once, and then flopped down like he'd run a marathon. I wished I could be like him, blissfully unaware of how his world had changed just like that. My clueless, fearless, hopelessly sweet dog.

A long time later, there was a knock on my door.

"KID!"

I rolled over and put a pillow over my head.

"KID, YOU DECENT? I'M COMING IN."

I heard the muffled sounds of Ace shuffling over to my bed and lowering himself until he was sitting next to me. I felt Ace-the-dog begin wagging his whole body and Ace-the-grandpa giving him some rough thumps on the back. Ace-the-grandpa lifted the pillow off my head and leaned in.

"Don't say it," I told him.

"SAY WHAT?"

"'I'm sorry.' 'It'll be okay.'"

"I'M NOT SORRY. IT WON'T BE OKAY."

"Very funny, Grandpa. It's just, I hate that stuff. It doesn't make it any better."

"WHO DO YOU THINK YOU'RE TALKING TO?"

He had a point. Ace-the-grandpa sat by my side. He scratched Ace-the-dog's ears and for once didn't try to bend mine.

"I didn't even get to say goodbye to her. Neither did Ace," I told him.

"SOMETIMES YOU DON'T," said Ace.

I rolled over and looked at him cautiously.

"Did you say goodbye to her?" I asked.

"TO THE STANLEYS' DOG?"

"No! To Bubbles."

"I did," Ace told me, his voice dropping to almost a whisper. "Maybe a thousand times. With what she had, we saw it coming a long way off." He shrugged. "But you know what? It never feels like enough."

I nodded. I thought about how Mrs. Stanley had said that Bridgie couldn't get comfortable anymore. How she howled because her world was too quiet and dark and confusing. Maybe Mr. and Mrs. Stanley saw this coming a long way off. Maybe they said goodbye to her a thousand times.

And maybe they were also wishing for a thousand and one. Just like me and Ace.

CHAPTER 14

I had a hard time falling asleep that night. I kept thinking about getting up and reading a book or something, but I wasn't quite awake enough to actually do it. But then all of a sudden I woke up and smelled something. Or maybe I woke up because I smelled something. This wasn't the first time I had been woken up by odors—having a poorly potty-trained puppy made this a fairly regular occurrence. This was a different smell. Sort of like something baking. No, not exactly. It reminded me of Sam singing "*I'll never leave your pizza burning. . . .*"

Pizza . . . burning . . . fire—

Was that smoke I smelled?

I threw off my blanket and ran to the door of my room, Ace hot on my heels. Remembering a "stop, drop, and roll" school assembly from years before, I cautiously touched the doorknob and was relieved to find it was cool. I grabbed Ace, threw the door open, and ran down the stairs, Ace's ears flapping as we dashed to safety.

My still-half-asleep plan was to race outside, where I supposed I'd find my frantic family. But as I sprinted into the kitchen, I heard the whir of the stove fan and—

"Auuughh!"

CRASH!!!

"OY YOY YOY!"

At the sound of my shriek, Ace, wearing his pajamas, a bathrobe, slippers, an apron, and oven mitts, had dropped the tray he was holding. Carrots, potatoes, and brown and black chunks of I'm not even sure what were scattered all over the floor. Ace wiggled out of my grasp and sprang to investigate. The whole mess was steaming, so he stood on the edge of the puddle, trying to figure out how to eat something that was too hot to touch. So hot it was practically—

"Oh no," I said.

Burning. That was what I'd smelled. What had I done?

"Grandpa, I'm sorry! I thought—"

"YOU THOUGHT WHAT?" barked Ace, his caterpillar eyebrows taking on an angry fighting stance.

It was going to sound so dumb, but I couldn't think of anything else to tell him except the truth: "I smelled something burning, so I thought—"

"YOU THOUGHT I WAS BURNING THE HOUSE DOWN?"

"I'm sorry," I whispered. "What were you making?"

"TZIMMES," he said. Then he began to chuckle. Then really laugh. "I ENDED UP MAKING A TZIMMES ALL RIGHT."

I looked at him, confused.

"*TZIMMES*," he explained, "MEANS 'STEW.' SO I STARTED OUT MAKING TZIMMES FOR THE STANLEYS. BUT *TZIMMES* ALSO MEANS 'A BIG MESS' OR 'A FUSS'."

I did my best to help Ace, crouching down with the dustpan while he attempted to sweep the tzimmes in the direction of the target. From this position, I could see that the brown parts were meat and the black parts were—no big surprise—prunes. Ace felt that any meal could be improved by adding prunes.

"Why are you making stew for the Stanleys?" I asked.

"IT'S WHAT YOU DO," said Ace. "LOOK, WE NEED TO START OVER, AND WE DON'T HAVE MUCH TIME." He began pulling things out of cupboards. Pots and pans, cinnamon and spices. "GET THE SOUR CREAM," he ordered. "EGGS. MILK. BUTTER. AND GET ME A CHAIR. HUSTLE, KID."

"Grandpa, it's"—I squinted at the clock—"three a.m. Can't this wait until tomorrow?" I asked.

"SOMETIMES IT IS BETTER TO BEG FORGIVENESS THAN TO ASK PERMISSION," said Ace. "YOU KNOW WHO SAID THAT?"

"You're not supposed to be using the stove, are you?" I replied.

"YOUR MOTHER WORRIES TOO MUCH," said Ace.

I couldn't argue with that.

"What are you making now?" I asked.

"YOUR GRANDMA BUBBLES' FAMOUS NOODLE KUGEL."

"Grandpa, you know the Stanleys aren't Jewish, right?"

"EVERYBODY LOVES KUGEL!" he insisted. "IT'S LIKE JEWISH LASAGNA."

For emphasis, he dumped a container of sour cream in a big bowl that appeared to have milk, eggs, and sugar in it. It looked like a wet, white, slimy mess. It did not look like any lasagna I'd ever seen, Jewish or otherwise. Then he rolled up his sleeves, and before I could stop him—

"Grandpa, what are you—"

He grabbed both my hands and plunged them deep into the bowl of cold, slimy goo. At which point I realized there were noodles in there too.

"WHAT DOES IT NEED?" demanded Ace.

"Fewer hands?" I said.

"WISE GUY," said Ace. "WHAT ELSE?"

I wiggled my fingers slowly. The mush felt cool and slippery. Ace let go, but he didn't take his hands out of the bowl. Instead, he moved them in circles, like they were mixing spoons, the goop slipping through his speckled, gnarled old-person fingers.

"More eggs?" I tried again. "Sour cream?"

"AND?" he repeated. "WHAT'S THE MOST IMPORTANT SEASONING, THE ONE THAT MAKES ALL THE DIFFERENCE?"

The most important seasoning? I closed my eyes and thought about Bubbles making noodle kugel. She carefully brushed butter on the top of it before putting it in the oven, using a thick wooden brush she kept in a kitchen drawer so it wouldn't get mixed up with her paintbrushes. Even so, she looked like a painter when she had a brush in hand, and Ace would always say "NOW *THAT* IS A WORK OF ART" when Bubbles slipped on her oven mitts and took the burbling, brown-crusted, cinnamon-good-smelling casserole out of the oven.

"COME ON, KID. THINK."

"Butter? Brown sugar?" I guessed.

"TZEDAKAH," he said.

"The Japanese girl?" I asked.

"WHO?"

"Sadako. We read a book about her at school."

Now it was Ace's turn to look confused.

"She was this girl," I said quickly. "This Japanese girl who got sick and wished she'd get better, and she tried to fold a thousand origami cranes so her wish would come true."

"SO?"

"So what?"

"SO NU? WHAT HAPPENED?"

"Sadako folded six hundred and forty-four paper cranes." I wished I hadn't started telling him, because all of a sudden, it made me think of Bubbles. She had cancer like Sadako. And Bubbles didn't get her miracle, either. "Her friends folded the rest after she died," I said quickly. "It's a true story. There's a statue of her in Japan."

Ace nodded. It seemed like maybe he was thinking about Bubbles too; that's how quiet he was. Ace said, "EXACTLY. THAT'S TZEDAKAH."

Remembering what Jeremy had said about O.J., I said, "I don't think so, Grandpa. Jeremy says *tzedakah* means 'spare change.'"

Ace shook his head. "YOU TELL JEREMY IT'S NOT THE MONEY. OR THE CRANES OR THE KUGEL, FOR THAT MATTER. TZEDAKAH IS WHAT YOU GIVE OF YOURSELF TO MAKE ALL THOSE THINGS MEAN SOMETHING."

I was tempted to point out that "Jewish lasagna" didn't have anything to do with Japanese origami birds or an old orange juice jug full of coins. Instead, I sprinkled some more brown sugar—and a healthy dose of tzedakah—on top.

Just like Bubbles used to.

In the morning, Mr. Stanley called to invite our whole family over for what he called "a little wake of sorts." "Nothing fancy," he added. "Come if you can."

"What's a wake?" I asked my mom when I hung up the phone.

"IT'S SHIVAH, ONLY WITH DRINKS," announced Ace, who never missed an opportunity to provide definitions.

"Not exactly," said my mom. "It's a Christian tradition. People get together after a loved one dies to pay their respects."

"So, Grandpa's right. It is like shivah."

"ONLY WITH BOOZE," added Ace.

"Dad!" said my mom sharply.

"WHAT?" said Ace innocently. "THAT'S JUST HOW IT IS. THEY DRINK, WE EAT."

My mom gave Ace a look. But she didn't correct him.

"Zelly, come in! You're our first guest," said Mrs. Stanley.

"My family will be here later, but my mom told me to bring this early so you could warm it up. It's called kugel," I explained, handing her the glass pan. It was wrapped in foil and secured by Ace with several rubber bands. "My grandpa and I made it. He calls it Jewish lasagna."

"That sounds delicious," said Mrs. Stanley. I hesitated for a moment, wondering if I should go home and come back, but Mrs. Stanley said, "Any chance I could rope you into staying here and helping me set up? Bob ran out to the store, and guests should be arriving any minute."

"Sure." I kicked my boots off, then stood awkwardly in the Stanleys' front hall while Mrs. Stanley excused herself to go set the coffeepot up. I'd never really spent any time at their house. Usually, I would grab Bridget at the door to take her out and deliver her back to the same spot. I glanced into the Stanleys' living room and noticed something surprising. When Mrs. Stanley returned carrying an oversized coffeepot, she saw where I was looking and shook her head.

"That's all Bob," she explained. "He puts the tree up the day after Thanksgiving every year. At least last year he went out and splurged on an artificial one. Before that, we'd end up with needles all over the carpet by the first week in December! Bob loves having Christmas as long as possible. I just let him go crazy and stay out of his way."

"It's really pretty," I told her. There were all different kinds of ornaments: shiny colored balls, glistening snowflakes, carved angels, even a tiny folded paper crane—and beagles. Many, many beagles. There were easily a couple of dozen hound dogs on the tree. Round ornaments with pictures of beagles, little china statues of beagles, a BEAGLE CROSSING sign, and even what appeared to be a beagle made out of bread dough.

"Are those all Bridgie?" I asked.

Mrs. Stanley chuckled. "No," she said. "Bob's had beagles ever since he was a boy, and we've had many beagles over the years while our kids were growing up. Each of the pups we've had has at least one ornament. Some have a whole bunch. Let me see if I can find Bridgie's."

She walked around the tree hunting for it. It was a small oval frame with a photograph of a beagle puppy in it. On the back, someone had written the words *Merry Christmas* and a date.

"Wow," I said. "She was six years older than me."

Mrs. Stanley nodded. I followed her into the kitchen, then helped her carry soda, juice, and quite a few bottles of wine into the dining room. She added two big bottles—one clear and one brown—from their liquor cabinet and went to fill a bowl up with ice. Maybe Ace was right about wakes after all.

"Bridgie was a treasure," said Mrs. Stanley. "We're going to miss her something terrible."

Mrs. Stanley began to cut up a ring-shaped cake. She looked like she was going to cry.

"She loved having you take her for walks, Zelly. I hope you know that."

"I'm going to miss her too. So is Ace."

"Ohhhh, Ace. That little rascal picked up her spirits in her twilight years, that's for sure. You know she'll be watching over him." Mrs. Stanley passed me a plate of assorted cookies and a stack of colorful paper napkins.

I hadn't thought about that. Bridget was up there with Bubbles now. Even though Bubbles preferred cats and didn't believe in pets, I could picture the two of them spending time together and becoming friends. That was a happy thought.

"Definitely," I said. I set the cookie tray on the table. Then I picked out one for myself and took a bite.

"And you know she'll be looking down and cheering when he passes his obedience test."

"Yeah, I'm not so sure about the passing part," I told her, but the doorbell rang, so Mrs. Stanley hurried to answer it.

The ornamental beagles stared at me from the tree. All of them, including Bridget, gave me knowing looks back.

Neither are we, they seemed to say.

CHAPTER 15

The day of Ace's test had been coming up for so long it didn't seem like it would ever arrive. December was a million years away. And then, all of a sudden, it was December first. Then December fourth.

Then December eighth: one day to go.

I slept terribly that night, worse than before any test I'd ever had for school. And every time I woke up during the night, I looked for Ace and found him snoozing happily. *Must be nice*, I thought. *To not know or care what was coming your way*. Because even if he had known, he would have wagged his tail at the idea. He loved seeing his dog friends at class, even Rosie, who didn't want to get anywhere near him. Ace loved the treats and hearing that he was a good boy. But he still seemed to love it when he messed up too. For him, it was all one big game. So if I gave him the command and marched away only to turn and find him right behind me, he'd be wagging his whole body, beaming up at me as if to say *Gotcha!*

"Today's the big day, huh?" said my dad the next morning at breakfast.

"Ugh," I answered. My mom brought me a bowl of oatmeal, but I pushed it away. "I'm not hungry," I told her.

"Oh?"

"Yeah. Actually, maybe I should just go back to bed?"

My mom put the underside of her wrist to my forehead and stared into space for a moment. Then she shook her head. "You're cool as a cucumber," she said. "I'll make you some tea, but you're going to school."

On my way out the door, my dad encouraged me to think of school as a "welcome distraction" from my dog obedience worries. Instead, it was the other way around, but without the welcome part. All day long, I couldn't stop thinking about the test. I rehearsed it in my head, tracing my pencil eraser along my desk slowly like it was on a leash. Heel, sit, down, stay, come. My pencil eraser, even with no practice, was a model of obedience. Too bad I couldn't take the test with it instead of Ace.

After school, I took Ace for a long walk, both to practice and to tire him out. I figured if he was exhausted, doing things like sitting, lying down, and staying in one place would sound extra-attractive. Plus he'd lack the energy to mount a full-scale doggie disobedience disaster.

When it was time to go, I clipped Ace-the-dog's leash on and went to knock on Ace-the-grandpa's door. No answer. I knocked again.

"Grandpa?"

"NU? COME IN ALREADY."

I turned the handle and opened the door. Ace was watching the local news on TV.

"Are you ready?" I asked him.

"AM *I* READY? THE QUESTION IS, IS *HE* READY?"

"Ready as he's going to be," I said. Which was true. "Whether that's ready enough remains to be seen."

"HE'LL DO FINE, KID. ZORG ZIG NICHT. I LOOK FORWARD TO HEARING ALL ABOUT HIS VICTORY."

"I'm not worried," I answered, like I always did when he told me to zorg zig nicht. "But what do you mean, hearing about it? You're not going?"

Ace tried unsuccessfully to look nonchalant. "NAH, I THINK I'LL STAY HOME FOR A CHANGE."

"Yeah, right," I said. But when he didn't budge, I stared at him in disbelief. "You're serious? You're not going? Why?"

"I'D RATHER NOT SAY," said Ace.

"You can't not say! We've been working on this for months, Grandpa. You're not just going to quit."

"IT'S NOT LIKE THAT, KID," said Ace. "LET'S JUST SAY A CERTAIN LADY FRIEND OF MINE HAS LET IT BE KNOWN THAT I SHOULD 'GIVE HER SOME SPACE.' IN DEFERENCE TO HER WISHES, I THINK IT WOULD BE BEST IF I BOWED OUT TONIGHT," said Ace, turning his gaze back to the screen, where the weatherman was pointing to a map of Vermont and New Hampshire.

"What? Mrs. Wright? When did you talk to her? What

did she say?" My heart started to beat double time. *Oh no*, I thought. *Was this because of what I said to her about Ace?*

"If you must know, kid," he said, not yelling for once, "she said she was starting to develop feelings for me. I know that might seem hard to believe, but there you have it. And for whatever reason, she seems to think it would be better if we didn't spend time together."

Because of me, I thought. Which made me sad. Because I was no longer sure I didn't want Mrs. Wright dating my grandpa.

"Do you?" I asked him cautiously.

"Do I what?"

"Have feelings for her."

"WHAT KIND OF MESHUGGE QUESTION IS THAT?" His usual volume came back, like pushing the plus sign on a remote.

"It's okay if you do," I told him. "Admit it, you do."

"Even if I did," he said, volume back down again, "it's probably for the best. I can't do . . . *this*. I'm an old dog. No new tricks left in me."

"You are *not* an old dog!" I shouted, surprised by the force of my response. "You're Ace, Grandpa. You can do anything! You dance merengue. You go to hot yoga class, for crying out loud!"

"*THIS* IS DIFFERENT, KID," said Ace, looking flustered. "I MIGHT BE ABLE TO PICK UP A DANCE MOVE OR TWO. BUT A RELATIONSHIP? THAT IS A DIFFERENT ANIMAL ALTOGETHER."

"In what way?" I asked.

"LOOK, KID," said Ace, "I APPRECIATE YOUR HELP, BUT THE POINT IS MOOT. SHE SAID TO GIVE HER SPACE. SO SPACE SHE GETS. YOUR MOTHER CAN DRIVE YOU, YES?"

"I guess," I said. I was really tempted to keep arguing, even though that was never a great strategy with Ace. Mrs. Wright just didn't want to get her heart broken, after all. And come to think of it, I had pretty much told her if she went out with Ace, she would. Fine, I decided. Maybe I could get there early, or stay late and talk to Mrs. Wright instead. I could convince her to give Ace another chance. I could remind her of all the reasons she liked him in the first place.

Since our car was no longer in the shop, my mom had already agreed to give us a ride. Sam came along, but he looked, well, awful. The reason was, a couple of nights earlier, the unthinkable had happened. Susie-the-whale had sprung yet another leak, but a titanic one this time, and all of her insides, which turned out to be tan nylon stockings, came spilling out her side like she had been harpooned. Mom tried to patch her again, but the fabric was so frayed at this point that she sat Sam down and talked to him about saying goodbye to Susie. Sam cried a lot, but after she agreed to buy him a new "big boy" whale, he finally said okay. Or so Mom claimed.

In the car, Mom turned on the radio, but then she cranked the heat so high we pretty much couldn't hear it in the back. Sam sat sullenly in his booster seat, slurping on the wrist of his disgusting robe.

"Any idea when the test will be over?" asked my mom.

"Nope," I said. "Maybe an hour or two? There are twelve dogs that need to take it."

"Mom?" whined Sam softly. With the heat and the music, I wasn't sure my mom heard him until she said, "Yes, sweetie?"

"I want Susie."

"Oh, honey."

"I want her . . . big. Like before."

"I know, sweetie. We talked about that, remember?"

I looked over at Sam, who nodded morosely. Now *that* was what I called grieving. Tears ran down his face, and he looked like he'd never be happy again in a million years. If he weren't wearing the most disgusting bathrobe on the planet, I might even have reached over and hugged him. That's how pathetic he looked.

"Mom?" asked Sam again.

My mom's eyes connected with his in the rearview mirror. "Uh-huh," she said.

"Did you throw her away?"

"I . . . I mean, I threw what was left of her away, sweetie, yes. I can show you when we get home. Her stuffing all fell out, and she was so old and worn there wasn't really much of her left anymore."

Sam was quiet for a minute, absorbing this. I almost thought he fell asleep, the car was so warm and everything. And then, "Mom? Can I have . . . what's left of her?"

"Um, we'll have to see, hon. I guess when we get home, I can go through the trash and try to find a piece that's salvageable. . . ."

But Sam was already asleep. He dropped off as soon as she said *I guess*. With all the noise in the car, he probably thought she said yes.

After being dropped off, I walked Ace up and down the block, just to make sure he got his last nervous peeing taken care of. He sniffed enthusiastically, checking out which of his buddies had already been there and left messages in the snow.

"Come on, Ace!" I said, shivering and giving his leash a yank. "Let's get this over with."

And then, to my utter and complete amazement, Ace marched over to a tree . . .

. . . and lifted his leg.

"Ace!" I said in surprise. "Good boy!" I couldn't believe it. He finally did it!

Maybe this was some kind of a sign. Maybe tonight would be the night he'd show off everything he could do!

When I walked in with Ace-the-dog, Mrs. Wright was already testing one of the other dogs. In a little while, she came over to me. "Hi, Zelly," she said. "Where's your grandpa?"

"He's at home," I said.

"Oh," said Mrs. Wright. "Everything okay?"

"Uh-huh," I told her, even though I wanted to say so much more. Starting with the fact that my grandpa was not an old dog. I wanted to remind her of how smart, and what a character, and, well, how *funny* he could be. And even though I had basically already forgiven Allie for what happened at the haunted house, I suddenly understood it for the first time. Allie wasn't feeling sorry for me. She was trying to make things better for me. Not for the wrong reasons—for the right ones. I wanted to pour it all right out there to Mrs. Wright. I wanted to say something like, *He actually has feelings for you, but he's just too afraid to admit it, because even an old person can be the new kid about this. He was married to Bubbles for almost forty-seven years, so you not being Bubbles is a big change for him.*

And then it hit me.

Afraid. Of change.

Ace was afraid of change.

But the other Ace was also afraid. Of *change*.

And just like that, I had an idea.

A completely crazy idea.

A so-completely-crazy-it-just-might-work idea.

So, what I said to Mrs. Wright was, "Can I go last? I think Ace needs to go to the bathroom."

I could have sworn Ace-the-dog gave me a confused look as I dragged him back outside, but he didn't exactly protest. I dug in my coat pocket and finally came up with my mom's cell phone. She had loaned it to me so I could call for a ride home. I scrolled through her recently dialed numbers until I found what I was looking for.

Ring . . . Ring . . .

Come on, I begged silently, cupping the phone to my ear while Ace, who seemed to have forgotten his new trick, squatted in the snow.

"HELLO?"

"Hi, it's me, Zelly."

"MARILYNN?"

"No, Grandpa. It's Zelly. I'm using my mom's phone. I'm at class. You know, for the test."

"SO NU? DID HE PASS?"

"That's just it. I need you here! And I forgot something at home, so you have to help me out." I was so desperate I even crossed my fingers and threw in a "Mrs. Wright says it's okay" for good measure.

There was no reply. So I took a deep breath and explained exactly what I needed him to bring. "Mom could drive you," I added.

"SHE'S PUTTING YOUR BROTHER TO BED. THAT'S OKAY, KID. I GOT IT ALL FIGURED OUT."

"You do? That's great!" I said. Then I remembered *all figured out* and added, "Wait, Grandpa, don't take the—"

Click.

"—bus," I said.

Ace and I went back inside and positioned ourselves off to one side. My hope was maybe Mrs. Wright wouldn't notice we had returned and that would buy Ace-the-Grandpa more time to get here. One by one, we watched Ace's classmates take the test. Some of them were pretty good, so I hoped Ace was paying attention. *Just do it like that,* I told him, *and everything will be fine.* Of course, Ace was too excited about the dogs walking by us while we waited. Each and every time, he sprang up, hoping his leash would magically disappear so he could join in the fun with whoever was closest.

It made me feel a little better to see that Ace wasn't the only one with this particular problem. Lady the Great Dane hated to lie down, so the minute her owner left the room, she popped back up like a jack-in-the-box. Mika the schnauzer did an impressive job staying down, but only because she fell asleep and didn't even notice when her owner came back. Cheeto, the yellow Lab puppy, tried to follow his owner out to the hall, and a beagle mix named Max *hooooowwwwwl*ed, reminding me fondly of Bridget. Mrs. Wright shook her head at poor Max, writing on her clipboard. I felt bad for Max's owner but also a little better for myself. *Mrs. Wright couldn't flunk everyone*, I reasoned. *Could she?*

Finally, Mrs. Wright pointed at me and motioned for me and Ace to come over. I looked around the room. Every other dog had completed the test.

I glanced at the door. No sign of Ace-the-grandpa. I closed my eyes and wished for him to magically appear.

I opened my eyes.

Bupkis.

"Zelly? It's time. You're up, kiddo," said Mrs. Wright.

I scrambled to my feet, my heart pounding. "Come on, Ace," I said out loud.

But in my head, I wasn't talking to my dog.

The test started out okay, even though I was nervous with everyone watching. Mrs. Wright said, "Ask your dog to sit," and before I even could, Ace sat. He wagged his tail but didn't jump up during the stranger-approach part, and he stayed good and down in his short stay. I saw Mrs. Wright making notes on her clipboard, but even that didn't spook me. Ace wasn't doing a perfect job, but he was doing good enough. Hopefully, this would help when we got to the long stay.

And then it was time for the final challenge. The way the long stay worked, I had to leave the room and Ace had to continue to stay where I had put him until I came back and gave him the release command. We'd practiced a million times at home, but Ace had never successfully pulled it off. He always, always got up to look for me, frantically forlorn I was gone forever.

I squatted down to look at Ace eye to eye. Sweet Ace, who tried so hard to be good, yet still couldn't help being so very, well, Ace. I locked eyes with him and tried to mentally convey everything I was feeling at that very moment: *Hey, buddy. I know it makes you crazy when I walk away, because it makes you feel like I'm never going to come back for you, and maybe it even makes you feel like you're going to end up back at the shelter again instead of living at our house. But I promise I'll be back. As soon as the two minutes are up and they let me back in. But you've got to trust me, Ace, because if you hop up and run around trying to find me, you'll flunk the test, and then, well, I don't know but it definitely won't be good. So please, please, please . . .*

But just as I was about to put Ace into his long stay and say a little prayer to anybody who might happen to be listening, the door opened.

In walked Ace.

Ace-the-grandpa, that is.

Without even acknowledging me, or Ace-the-dog, or Mrs. Wright, he crossed the room and sat down—still wearing the Baxter State—in a folding chair. Just as I had requested, he was carrying something familiar in his arms.

An old plastic orange juice jug with a face drawn on it.

The one "dog" who *always* stayed right where you put him. O.J.

Ace-the-grandpa stared at Ace-the-dog.

Ace-the-dog stared at O.J.

Hrnnnn, whined Ace softly, remembering The Awful Noise.

"Zelly?" said Mrs. Wright, ignoring Ace-the-grandpa's entrance. "We're waiting, dear."

"Ace," I said out loud, but the first Ace I looked at wasn't my dog. I stared at Ace-the-grandpa and silently willed him to behave. *Sit*, I thought. *Stay*. *And above all, DO NOT shake O.J.*

I willed all of the same things at Ace-the-dog.

"Stay, Ace," I said.

Then I turned and walked out of the room.

CHAPTER 16

Those were the longest two minutes of my life.

When Mrs. Wright came out to the hall to get me, I felt this giddy jolt of excitement. *Maybe he did it. Maybe Ace finally did it. Maybe Ace sat. And stayed. And passed!*

I opened the door and saw:

Ace-the-grandpa on his feet, facing off with Ace-the-dog. Definitely not sitting.

Ace-the-dog on his feet, his back to the door. Definitely not staying.

And all over the floor, in every direction:

Money.

Dimes and quarters and nickels and dollar bills and lots and lots of pennies.

Then I noticed what Ace-the-dog had in his mouth:

O.J.

His feet were planted in his favorite tug-of-war stance. As were Ace-the-grandpa's feet, since he was holding on firmly to the leash I used to walk O.J. with.

"Ace, NO!" I yelled.

Both Aces turned to look at me.

"DROP!" I ordered.

And, miraculously, Ace-the-dog suddenly dropped O.J., who landed with a thud because many of the coins were still inside of him.

I marched over and grabbed O.J. by the handle, then Ace by the leash. I could feel the tears coming, which made everything worse. I stormed out into the hall and sat down in the stairwell. Ace smiled at me and threw his wiggling, licking self at me, doggily clueless and thrilled to pieces to see me. *Oh boy, you're back!* He grinned gleefully. "Ace, you don't understand," I told him, even though I was grateful he wanted to cheer me up. Or maybe he just liked the salty taste of my tears.

Through the glass window on the door, I saw everyone filing out of the auditorium, leading their dogs, talking, laughing, and carrying certificates. I could see Ace and Mrs. Wright talking—which was what I wanted, but not like this. In my head, it had gone differently. My dream had been that Ace-the-dog would see O.J., remember The Awful Noise, and decide to actually stay, for a change.

Ace came out in a few minutes. No certificate, just a little slip of paper that looked like it could be one of Hailey Larson's sleepover party invitations. Ace held it out to me.

"No thanks," I said. I couldn't even look at it. Ace raised one eyebrow, but he folded it up and put it in his pocket.

"AND," said Ace, digging in his other pocket. He took my hand and deposited a big handful of money in it. I guess he'd collected O.J.'s contents off the floor.

"GELT BY ASSOCIATION," he joked.

"Yeah, it's all just one big joke," I said. "You don't get it."

"WHAT DON'T I GET?"

"Forget it," I said. "Let's go."

"PUT YOURSELF IN HIS SHOES, KID."

"He doesn't have shoes! He's a dog!"

"I GOT NEWS FOR YOU, KID. EVERYBODY HAS SHOES." Ace stood, hitched his pants up over his belly, and led the way outside.

"Yeah? Well, what about *my* shoes? I worked for months on training, just so I could have a sleepover. I did my best, and where did it get me? Nowhere! And not only that, I passed up an invitation to go to a sleepover to come here instead!"

"ALL RIGHT, SO YOUR SHOES STINK," admitted Ace.

"I know!" I told him as we carefully navigated the icy parking lot. "Wait, how did you get here?" I asked, remembering that Ace had arrived late.

"I FINAGLED A MEANS OF TRANSPORTATION," replied Ace. He walked up to a yellow Volkswagen "punch-buggy-no-punch-back," as Sam would say. The back end of it was covered—I mean completely wallpapered—with bumper stickers. Some were ones I'd seen before, like I LOVERMONT and LOVE YOUR MOTHER, with a picture of the earth. Others had slogans like WELL-BEHAVED WOMEN RARELY MAKE HISTORY and UPPITY WOMEN UNITE. There must have been a hundred of them, easy. *The coolest car on the planet*, I suddenly remembered, according to Sam.

Ace unlocked the passenger side and held the seat down for me and Ace to jump in back.

"You borrowed Margie's car?" I asked. "Aren't you supposed to not drive anymore?"

"YOU'D RATHER TAKE THE BUS?"

I got in the car. Ace pulled out of the parking lot and headed home without saying another word. But for some reason, when he got to our street, instead of turning right, he kept going straight.

"Grandpa? That was our street."

"YOU KNOW WHAT I DO WHEN MY SHOES STINK?" he asked. "COME ON. I'M GOING TO SHOW YOU."

"That's okay," I told him. "My shoes are actually fine. Let's just go home."

"THREE LEFTS AND WE'LL BE RIGHT THERE," he answered.

"Grandpa, I just—" He turned left into a long driveway. I looked around as he veered left up the winding path and then a steep hill. "The golf course?" I asked. "What are we doing at the golf course?"

"I COME HERE," Ace said.

"In the winter?"

"YUP. CLEARS MY HEAD."

I remembered when Ace had his accident. *What was he doing at the golf course?* my dad had asked. Ace had always loved golf, but he stopped playing when Bubbles died and he moved in with us. Plus everyone knew that as soon as the snow fell, the golf course was only good for one thing:

Sledding.

Ace turned left into a parking spot at the top of the sledding hill and got out. Reluctantly, I followed him, leaving Ace-the-dog in the car, where he was already fast asleep, exhausted from his big night. Since it was after dark, there was no one else there. A round golden moon was out, though, so the snow-covered hill practically glowed. You could see icy tracks where kids like Sam and me had been flying down the hill since the first snows in November, narrowly missing the trees positioned dangerously at the bottom.

Ace closed his eyes and took a deep breath. He spread his arms wide and exhaled. "AHHHHH!" he bellowed. Next he used his cane to pick up a blue plastic sled someone had apparently left there. Holding it vertically, Ace began doing some sort of limbering-up stretches. Was the full moon to blame? This was crazy!

"Grandpa, stop!" I blurted out. "You're acting crazy! There are better ways to deal with your grief. You don't have to break every rule!"

"BETTER WAYS TO DEAL WITH MY . . . WHAT?"

"Grief," I repeated quietly. "Mrs. Wright says you're acting this way because you're grieving. Did she tell you that?"

"NO. WHAT ELSE DID SHE SAY?"

"She says it's okay. And if going dancing makes you feel good, maybe you need to go dancing."

"SHE'S A SMART COOKIE, THAT ONE," he said.

I nodded. It didn't make me mad to hear him say it. I was pretty sure even Bubbles, up on her cloud with Bridget, was nodding in agreement too.

"It's okay if you like her," I told him.

"ISSAT SO?"

"But you're not going to be around to tell her if you go through with this. This is totally meshugge!"

"WHAT IS TOTALLY MESHUGGE?"

"Sledding," I said.

Ace laughed out loud, a big belly laugh. It turned into a coughing fit, as was often the case. When he finally stopped laughing and coughing, he said, "ZELDALEH, LISTEN TO ME: I DO MANY THINGS. MAYBE SOME THINGS I DO I SHOULDN'T DO. BUT THERE'S ONE THING I DON'T DO: SLED."

"You don't?"

"ARE YOU FOR REAL? ON THE ICE, ON MY TUCHES? WHAT KIND OF A MESHUGGENER DO YOU THINK I AM?"

I felt a gigantic sense of relief. I looked out over the steep frozen hill. "Well, then, what are we doing here? Why do you go to the golf course in the winter?"

"TO TALK TO HER."

"Who?"

"MERYL STREEP. WHO DO YOU THINK? YOUR GRANDMA!"

"Bubbles is buried at the golf course?" I asked.

"NO, KID," said Ace. "WE USED TO PLAY THIS COURSE TOGETHER, ALMOST EVERY WEEKEND. . . ." Ace's voice trailed off. He cleared his throat. "WHAT CAN I SAY? I MISS HER, ALL RIGHT?" Then he added, "PLUS IT'S QUIET HERE. SO I KNOW SHE CAN HEAR ME."

I couldn't help laughing at that. "Grandpa," I told him, "no one ever has a problem hearing you."

"YOU IN THE MARKET FOR A POTCH IN TUCHES, KID?" he asked me.

"Nope, I'm all set," I said. But I smiled. Only Ace could make me feel better by suggesting I deserved a smack on the bottom.

"SO?"

"So, what?"

"SO WE'RE HERE, ALREADY. TELL HER SOMETHING."

"Like what?"

"LIKE THIS." Ace handed me a piece of paper. I unfolded it and held it out to try to read it by the light of the moon. It was what Ace had received at the end of his test.

Some of the writing was hard to read. But there at the bottom in big letters were the words:

CONDITIONAL PASS.

"Pass?" I whispered. "As in . . ."

"PASS AS IN PASS. NU?"

"Woo-hoo!" I hooted, throwing my arms around Ace and giving him a huge hug.

"CONDITIONAL," continued Ace, talking over my shoulder as he hugged me back, "AS IN HE NEEDS TO COME BACK AND REPEAT THE PART HE MESSED UP. BUT FOR NOW, HE'S AS GOOD AS GRADUATED."

"We did it!" I told him. And then, softly, I addressed the snow-covered hill and the trees and the stars in the sky—which I couldn't see, but in my heart, I knew they were there. Somewhere, hiding behind Bubbles' and Bridget's clouds. "Grandma," I said shyly. "Bubbles, we did it," I said.

"SHE DID IT," corrected Ace, his arm draped around my shoulder. "KID, YOU SHOULD'VE SEEN YOUR GRANDDAUGHTER IN ACTION. GOOSE BUMPS, I TELL YOU!" He kissed me on the head and gave me a proud squeeze. "AND SPEAKING OF GOOSE BUMPS, ENOUGH FREEZING OUR TUCHESES OFF. LET'S GET A MOVE ON."

"Did you just call Bubbles *kid*?" I asked him.

Ace nodded. "ALWAYS," he said.

"But you call me *kid*," I said. I had never liked it much. Until now.

"I COULD CALL YOU SOMETHING ELSE," said Ace. "RUTABAGA?" he suggested. "PICKLE NOSE?"

"Let's stick with *kid*," I told him.

Ace barked excitedly as we climbed back into the car. He flung himself at me, slurping my face with doggie kisses, all signs of obedience vanished.

But it didn't matter—Ace had passed.

Poor old battered O.J. sat in the front seat to protect him from further attacks. I couldn't resist reaching over the seat and giving him a little pat. *Sorry*, I told him silently. *And thanks*.

Don't mention it, kid, he told me back, smiling as always.

CHAPTER 17

"Out!" My dad paused in the kitchen doorway, wielding a pastry bag filled with neon-green frosting.

"Come on, can't I just peek? Please?" I asked, leaning from side to side, trying to glimpse the cake he was decorating.

"Yahh! Slime her!!!" begged Sam, who was thrilled to be on the other side of the door, hopped up on buttercream icing and green dye. Ace barked excitedly, skittering across the kitchen floor, hoping food would be flying soon. He looked great. As a special treat, Mom had taken him to the Poochie Palace dog salon to get him ready for the party. My sleepover party.

"Sam's going to Paul's, right?" I asked my dad.

"Zelly, we've been over this already. He'll be here until seven, then Paul's dad will pick him up. He won't be here for the sleepover part."

"But my party starts at seven," I reminded him. I loved saying those words: *my party!*

"Right," said my dad coolly. "So I suppose it is *possible* your friends might see your brother for five minutes before he gets whisked away."

"What about Ace?" I asked.

"I believe his plans for the evening were to watch television in his room."

"But I need the TV," I said nervously. "We're going to want to watch a movie."

"Zelly, would you please stop? We've been over this. The TV is on a rolling cart. We can easily move it into the living room for you and your friends later on."

"Okay, okay," I said. It was going to be the best sleepover ever!

When my dad finally declared that the kitchen was no longer off-limits, I went to look for the Sally's Pizza menu. I found Ace poking around under the roasted chicken we'd had for dinner the night before with a butter knife. As I pulled open the junk drawer, Ace dipped his knife into the gooky mess under the chicken and spread it on the slice of rye bread he was holding.

"What are you doing?" I asked.

"WHAT? HAVING A LITTLE NOSH."

"Did you just put . . . chicken juice on your toast?"

"SCHMALTZ," Ace corrected me. "WANT A BITE?"

I recoiled in disgust. "Are you supposed to be eating that?" I asked him.

"ARE YOU SUPPOSED TO BE GETTING A SLEEPOVER?" he shot back.

He had a point. When Ace and I came home to show off Ace's conditional pass, Mom and Dad were pleased, but their idea was that the sleepover could wait until Ace retook the test and got a full pass.

"But, Mom," I wailed, so frustrated I couldn't see straight. "I did everything right! And Ace did almost everything right!"

"Exactly," said my mom gently. "Almost everything."

"COUNSELOR, LET ME SEE THAT DOCUMENT," demanded Ace, holding out his hand. I unpinned my proposal from the bulletin board and passed it to him.

"That's so not fair!" I said. "You promised I could have a sleepover if he passed. A conditional pass is a pass!"

"Zelly, he's come a long way, but he's not quite there yet. So maybe in another month or two—"

"CAN *YOU* MAKE THAT DOG STAY?"

"Dad, do you mind?" said my mom.

"CAN YOU?" Ace demanded.

"I don't know," Mom admitted.

"EXACTLY," said Ace triumphantly. "HOW CAN YOU REQUIRE THE KID TO DO SOMETHING THAT YOU YOURSELF CAN'T DO?"

"Lynn," said my dad in his *I can see where this is going* voice. My mom ignored him.

"I didn't sign on to train the dog," she told Ace. "Zelly did, and what I'm trying to do is hold her to her end of the bargain."

"GO ON. TRY." Ace sat down. I did too. "I'VE GOT A NICKEL SAYS YOU CAN'T DO IT."

"I've got a whole orange juice jug full of nickels," I added. I had argued with Ace a million times, but this was the first time I had been on the same side with him.

"This is ridiculous," said my mom.

"YOU WANNA KNOW WHY?" asked Ace.

"No, but I'm sure you're going to—"

"HE'S NOT READY," said Ace. "SOMETIMES YOU CAN'T RUSH THESE THINGS."

"Like Sam," I chimed in. "He said he was ready to give up Susie, but he really wasn't. So you fished part of her skin out of the trash and let him keep it."

"YOU DID WHAT?" said Ace.

"That's not the same thing," said my mom.

"Yes, it is! It's not fair to punish me because Ace isn't ready to do this one thing yet. He's just a puppy."

"FROM EACH ACCORDING TO HIS ABILITY," announced Ace. "MARX," he added.

I wasn't sure which of the Marx Brothers said that, but I knew better than to ask at a critical time like this. Ace was arguing for me, not against me. And it seemed—though I could be wrong—like maybe we were winning.

"FURTHERMORE," said Ace, holding out the proposal, "WHAT WE HAVE HERE IS AN UNCONSCIONABLE CONTRACT."

"An unconscious what?" I asked.

"UNCONSCIONABLE," repeated Ace. "A CONTRACT

IS UNCONSCIONABLE IF IT IS UNJUST OR EXTREMELY ONE-SIDED IN FAVOR OF THE PERSON WHO HAS THE SUPERIOR BARGAINING POWER. AS SUCH, IT IS AN AFFRONT TO THE INTEGRITY OF THE JUDICIARY SYSTEM TO ENFORCE SUCH CONTRACTS."

"Huh?" I said.

"TAKE IT UNDER ADVISEMENT," suggested Ace, handing the proposal to my mom and giving her a stern judicial look. He was a big fan of taking things under advisement, which was judgespeak for "think about it."

"This court is adjourned," said Mom. I didn't like how that sounded. It reminded me of Shlomo losing his suit. I didn't want to lose my suit. Or my sleepover.

Which is why I couldn't have been more surprised when, at the grocery store the next day, my mom put a bag of Hershey's Kisses in our shopping cart. My eyebrows went up. Sam's did too.

"Whoa!" said Sam. Without missing a beat, he ran up the aisle, grabbed a box of Froot Loops, and held it up. "Can we get these too?"

"Whoa, yourself!" said my mom, disarming Sam and putting the cereal back on the shelf. "I haven't completely taken leave of my senses. The candy's for Zelly's party."

"Really?" I said.

My mom nodded. "Your father and I discussed this, and we think Ace has a point. You did do everything you could to get Ace trained. The last little bit, well, hopefully it'll come in time if you stick with it."

"I will," I told her.

"I thought you might. So I took the liberty of signing you up for another session of classes. And you'll be happy to know that your father's course finishes next week, so he can take you."

"Oh," I said. "Actually, that's okay. Ace and I sort of have the routine down now."

"B-but that's not fair!" said Sam. "Plus chocolate will make Ace die!"

"Sam," said my mom, "Zelly will make sure to keep the candy where Ace can't get it. And we'll put some aside for you, okay?"

"As long as we're getting candy, can we get some of those sour guys too?" I asked, not wanting to miss the rare time my mom actually bought candy. Halloween didn't count.

"Suit yourself," said Mom. "It's your party."

And now, a week later, it finally was my party. And for the most part, everything was going exactly as I wanted. Allie, Jenny, Megan, Simone, and the Wilson twins, Tasha and Talia, were going to sleep over. Hailey had a gymnastics meet the next morning, so she couldn't come, but she wanted to, which was the important thing—and I got to invite Simone because Hailey couldn't come. Plus we had all the right sleepover stuff, and my brother was going to leave any minute and be elsewhere overnight. Perfect!

Except for one thing: Ace-the-grandpa standing smack in the middle of everything, eating a chicken-juice sandwich, no less. And then, to make matters worse, he went to his room and came back with a silver menorah and a blue box of candles.

"Grandpa, what are you doing?"

"WHAT? IT'S THE FIRST NIGHT OF HANUKKAH."

"No, it's not. Hanukkah starts tomorrow, see?" I pointed at the calendar. Ace squinted at it like he had never noticed it before.

"THAT'S A SECULAR CALENDAR," he informed me. "JEWISH HOLIDAYS START THE NIGHT BEFORE. HANUKKAH STARTS TONIGHT."

"Grandpa, I think it starts tomorrow night. Plus I'm having a sleepover party tonight. So can you maybe put that stuff away?"

Ding-dong!

I glanced at the clock on the microwave. Six-twenty-seven. Hopefully, it was Paul's dad coming early to pick Sam up. It was finally time for my party, the one I had worked so hard to earn. I was not about to let anything stand in the way of it being perfect.

"I'll get it!" I yelled, running to answer the door.

"Heyyyy!" said Allie, grinning. She was holding a tote bag with a pillow sticking out of it, plus a stack of magazines topped with a giant candy cane tied with a ribbon.

"Thanks for coming early," I told her. Never having done this before, I was grateful for her sleepover expertise.

"No problem," said Allie. I led her in and showed her the living room, a.k.a. Sleepover Party Central.

"What do you think? I could spread these out, or maybe we should just leave them in a stack?" I potchked with the magazines, trying to figure out the best way to arrange them.

"Zelly, calm down. It looks amazing in here."

"Really?" I asked, hoping she wasn't just trying to make me feel good. I had given a lot of thought to making things perfect. There were bowls of chocolate kisses and sour gummies on the mantel, to keep Ace from repeating his Halloween performance. There were extra pillows and blankets piled in a corner, just in case anyone forgot their sleeping bags. And my parents had let me open one Hanukkah present early: a gift card to buy a whole bunch of music to play. Allie helped me pick songs, since she has an older sister to tell her what's in and what's out. There was popcorn to pop and a rainbow of nail polish. Allie plopped down her stuff and pulled out a big bag of nail salon supplies, and even I had to admit: it did look pretty perfect.

Ding-dong!

"I'll get it," I yelled again, running for the door. Allie followed me. Hopefully, it was Paul's dad arriving to pick up Sam. I threw open the front door.

Jeremy stood there, wearing his giant down jacket and a long blue scarf with the Red Sox emblem on it. Snow had just started falling and was clinging to his wavy hair and glasses. He was carrying a shoebox in his mittened hands.

"Happy Hanukkah!" he said.

CHAPTER 18

"Jeremy, what are you doing here?" I said desperately. "Hanukkah starts tomorrow night."

"No, it doesn't," said Jeremy. "Tonight's the first night. We already lit candles. I got this scarf. Here!" He handed the shoebox to me. "We made sufganiyot," he explained as I opened it and a delicious smell wafted out. "My mom made way too many, so she said I should bring some over to your family."

"Soof gani yot?" asked Allie.

"Jelly donuts," explained Jeremy, rubbing his hands together. "Can I come in? It's kind of cold out here."

"Oh!" I said. "Um, sure. For a sec." As Jeremy followed me and Allie to the kitchen, my mind was reeling. All the girls were going to show up any minute. This wasn't exactly the sleepover scene I'd planned.

"Jeremy! What a nice surprise." My mom came in carrying Sam's *Star Wars* sleeping bag.

"Happy Hanukkah," said Jeremy. "We had some extra sufganiyot, so I brought them over."

"How sweet of you," said my mom. "I feel so silly—we all thought Hanukkah started tomorrow night. But Ace found the menorah and we were just about to light the candles. Can you stay long enough to do the blessings with us?"

"I, uh . . ." Jeremy looked from me and Allie to my mom and back again. "Sure," he finally said.

Mom set the menorah on a cookie sheet lined with aluminum foil. In place already were two candles—a regular one plus one in the shammes position—that Sam had jammed in. The non-shammes one was green, short, and jutting off to the side precariously. The shammes, proud and tall, was blue.

"I get blue!" announced Sam.

"Big surprise," I said. "We always root for one candle or another to last the longest," I explained to Allie.

"Seth and I do too," said Jeremy. "I mean, we used to. Before Seth got all teenage and attitudey."

Allie giggled appreciatively, because she thought pretty much everything about Jeremy's older brother was cute. But before anyone else could weigh in on which candle should win—

Ding-dong!

Oh no! Trying to stay calm, I ran to get the door. "Hi, Zelly dear," said Mrs. Stanley. She was wearing a big shawl, and there was a light dusting of snow on her shoulders. The snow was coming down even harder than when Jeremy showed up. "Is this a bad time?" she asked.

"I, uh, no," I lied.

"I just wanted to stop by and tell you how much Bob and I appreciated the ornament you made. It looks just like her! You have to come help us find a place for it on our tree."

"Oh. Sure. You're welcome." For the longest time, Bubbles' painting kit had sat on my shelf. But after that night at the golf course, I lifted the lid and peeked inside. The smell still gave me a lump in my throat, but each time I opened it, the sadness wore off a little. And when I uncapped some of the tubes of paint, I discovered a shade that was the exact butterscotch color of Bridget's ears.

Just then, I noticed that Mrs. Stanley was holding something in her arms under her shawl. It was moving a little. Wiggling, in fact.

"I also wanted to introduce you to someone. I know it's really soon, but, well . . ."

A little beagley nose poked out. Followed by two tiny, floppy ears and two deep brown eyes.

"Awwwwww," I said reflexively.

"Maureen," I heard my mom say behind me. And then, "Oh, did you bring her? Let's have a look at— Awwwwww!"

"I know, isn't she darling?" said Mrs. Stanley.

"Come in for a minute, won't you?" said my mom. "It's really coming down!"

"Oh, I wouldn't want to impose," said Mrs. Stanley. "Plus Bob will worry if I don't get this little girl back soon."

"It's no trouble. We were just about to light Hanukkah candles. You can join us."

"Oh, well, just for a minute," said Mrs. Stanley.

"What's her name?" I asked.

"We're still trying to figure that out," said Mrs. Stanley. "Suggestions welcome!"

"Okay, where was I?" said my mom. "Right, matches."

Ding-dong!

WOOF! went Ace. *Yeep!* went the puppy, right on cue.

"WHAT IS THIS? GRAND CENTRAL STATION?" said Ace.

"I got it," I yelled again, running for the door.

Mrs. Wright stood on the front steps, Rosie in her arms.

"Hi, Zelly dear," she said.

"Zelly?" My mom came up behind me. "Can I help you?" she said to Mrs. Wright.

"I'm Delores Wright, Ace and Zelly's dog obedience teacher," said Mrs. Wright. "But I really came to see Ace. The person, not the dog," she added.

"Oh!" said Mom. "Won't you come in?"

"Thank you," said Mrs. Wright, following my mom into the kitchen.

"DELORES?" said Ace, wiping his hands on his pants.

"Hello, Ace," said Mrs. Wright.

Ruff! went Ace. *Yeep!* echoed the puppy.

Yap! Yap! went Rosie, staring at the puppy. She had something that seemed like envy on her furry little face.

"Allie!" I stage-whispered, pulling her into the living room. "What am I going to do? This is a disaster!"

"What is?"

"Everything is! All I wanted was a plain old regular sleepover party. Instead, I've got Grand Central Station!"

"Zelly, it'll be fine. You'll see."

I gave Allie a look. How could she not see what was going on? "Allie, be honest," I said. "Don't just try to make everything okay. Like with Hailey. I know about that."

"What are you talking about?" asked Allie.

"I know you got her to invite me to her sleepover because you feel sorry for me."

"That's not true."

"Oh yeah? Then why did you tell her all that stuff about my grandpa almost dying?"

"To get her to invite you, Zelly. Duh! But that's not why! I wanted you to come because her party would've been more fun with you there!"

"Fun, like funny, ha-ha?" I said suspiciously.

"Zelly! Fun like *fun*. What is *with* you tonight? Why are you being so weird?"

"I guess it runs in my family."

"Yeah? Well, I *like* your family," said Allie. "I'd trade in a heartbeat."

"*Pfft*," I said, rolling my eyes. "Your family is perfect. Your life is perfect."

Allie *pfft*ed me back. "*Perfect?* Please! Julia acts like I'm two and bosses me around, telling me what to do and not do, wear and not wear, like and not like. And my whole life is hand-me-downs. No one ever buys me anything new, not even a stupid magazine."

"That's not true. What about your new sweater with the pom-poms? Or that hoodie with the fleece lining?"

"Julia's and Julia's."

"Okay, fine. Your shoes stink too," I admitted.

"What?!" Allie looked down at her feet, alarmed.

I couldn't help smiling. "Not like that. It's just something Ace says."

Ding-dong!

"Great, who's next?" I said. "Nicky Benoit?"

"Oh, didn't I tell you I invited Naked-Mole-Rat Nicky?" joked Allie, giving me her best naked-mole-rat smile.

"Okay, you're right," I admitted. "That would be a whole lot worse. But, still, you've got to help me!"

"Help you what?" said Allie.

"Zelly!" called my mom. "Your friends are here."

Allie and I ran to the door, Ace at our heels. Jenny, Megan, and Simone stood on the front stoop, giggling in the falling snow. Across the street were the Wilson twins, hopping out of their dad's Subaru. The snowplow rumbled past them, filling our driveway with snow.

Jenny, Simone, Megan, Tasha, and Talia clomped into the kitchen, talking and laughing. They stopped and went silent when they saw the crowd gathered. But then Jenny spotted the puppy. "Awwwww, look!" she said, and there was a collective chorus of *awwwwwws*. All the girls dove under the table to admire the baby beagle. Rosie danced in circles, trying to steal a little attention, but it was no use. The puppy had her beat.

"Give her some room, okay?" I said. "Hey, why don't we go into the living room!" I grabbed Jenny's overnight bag from her and dragged all of the girls out of the kitchen. "Sour Patch, guys?" I offered, moving the bowls of treats to the coffee table to distract my guests.

"Who are all those people?" asked Megan, scooping up a handful of candy.

"Oh, nobody," I said, unwrapping a kiss. "Just my neighbor and my dog obedience teacher."

"Are those Ace's girlfriends?" asked Allie.

"What! No!" I said, alarmed.

"Not even the little one? She's so cute!"

Did she mean Mrs. Wright? I guessed so, since Mrs. Stanley was much bigger, but still. I gave Allie a sharp look to say *You're supposed to be helping me*. Plus this wasn't the first time she'd blown something she'd promised to keep secret.

"Wanna watch a movie?" I tried, mostly because I needed something, anything, to get their mind off the scene in the kitchen. Meanwhile, Paul's dad still hadn't appeared, and we could all hear talking and laughing.

"What's that smell?" asked Simone.

Smell? I was starting to panic. Ace hadn't left one of his little presents for us, had he? I had walked him earlier and my mom promised she'd keep an eye out, but clearly she was busy doing other things.

"Smell?" I said nervously, sniffing the air.

Jenny nodded too. "Yeah," she said.

"Like French fries," added Tasha.

It did smell like that, I had to admit, but that was ridiculous. Mom never made French fries. Her oven fries were tasty, but they didn't make the house smell like hot, sizzling grease. . . . *Oh no! Please tell me Ace wasn't heating up his beloved schmaltz.* I wouldn't put it past him. I pictured him pouring it over popcorn. . . .

Just then, my mom came in, drying her hands on a dish towel.

"Zelly, would you and your friends like to come in and join us while we light the Hanukkah candles?"

"No, Mom, we're fine!" I said, but before I could stop them, all of the girls except Allie hopped up and went back to the kitchen. "Mom!" I said in frustration.

"What?"

"What is Ace doing? He's ruining everything!"

"Ace?" My mom looked around quickly. "I thought he was in the kitchen. Did he leave a little present?"

"Mom, not Ace-the-dog. Grandpa! Did you say he could use the stove?"

"Look, Zelly," she said. "I think you should relax. Ace is behaving himself. Come see for yourself." She gave me a meaningful look.

"We'll be right there, Mrs. Fried," said Allie in her voice that grown-ups love.

"Thanks a lot," I said when my mom left the room. "I thought you were my best friend."

"I am!"

"Well, then, why did you say that thing about my grandpa's girlfriends?"

"What are you talking about?" asked Allie.

"When I told you about my grandpa having three girlfriends that we know of, remember how you promised not to tell anyone?"

"I didn't!"

"You so totally did! Right after you came in, you asked if those were Ace's girlfriends."

Allie started to laugh. "I meant Ace-the-dog!" she said. "Wouldn't he and that little beagle puppy be cute together?"

"Beagle?" I asked. "You meant Ace, not Ace?"

Allie nodded.

"Okay, I feel stupid now," I said.

"But, wait, *are* those your grandpa's girlfriends?"

I responded by throwing a pillow at Allie, which made me feel a lot better.

"Zelly, you know, there *is* one person who could make your party a disaster."

"Who, my grandpa? Sam? Jeremy?"

"Zelly."

"Yeah?"

"I mean *you*. If you keep on freaking out, you are going to ruin your own party! Seriously! Cut it out."

"Okay, okay," I said. I was pretty sure I wasn't the only one who would be capable of ruining the party.

But I could also see that maybe she had a point.

When Allie and I returned to the kitchen, we found everyone talking at once. My mom was handing mugs to Mrs. Wright and Mrs. Stanley, and I could smell cider with cinnamon sticks warming on the stove. Jenny, Megan, Simone, Jeremy, and the twins were sitting on the floor, playing with the dogs. My dad was grating potatoes, and so was Mrs. Stanley. Ace was frying potato pancakes—in vegetable oil, thank goodness, not chicken fat—and stacking them on piles of paper towels next to the stove. Paul and his dad had arrived too, and so had Mr. Stanley, and it seemed they were staying for latkes, because their coats were piled on a kitchen chair and Sam and Paul were having a lightsaber battle. "Not too near the stove, boys!" warned my mom.

"AH, ZELDALEH. THERE YOU ARE. GET O.J., WOULD YOU?"

"Why?" I asked suspiciously. I couldn't bear to put Ace-the-dog through a repeat performance of his obedience test.

"NOTHING TO DO WITH HIM," said Ace, like he could read my mind. "I PROMISE."

I opened my mouth to make an excuse, but the *No freaking out* look on Allie's face made me stop. So I went to my room and got O.J. When I returned, Ace turned the spatula over to my dad, wiped his hands on his apron, and took O.J. from me. Ace uncapped him and poured the change inside into a bowl that was sitting on the table. He left the room and came back with another small bowl—this one filled with net bags of chocolate coins—and a small object.

"YOU'RE PROBABLY WONDERING WHAT THIS TCHOTCHKE IS," he said.

"It's a dreidel," said Jeremy.

"I thought they were supposed to be made out of clay," said Megan.

"Yeah, like in that song we sing in the Christmas concert at school every year," added Jenny.

Ace pointed to the dreidel he was holding. "THESE ARE HEBREW LETTERS, AND EACH ONE REPRESENTS A WORD."

"*Nes gadol haya sham*," explained Jeremy. "It means 'A great miracle happened there.' "

"BUT EACH LETTER ALSO HAS A MEANING IN THE GAME," said Ace. "SO IF YOU SPIN AND YOU GET THIS ONE"—he pointed to a skinny letter—"NUN, YOU GET BUPKES."

"Nothing," I translated.

"FOR THIS ONE"—he pointed to a letter that looked almost the same but had a little heel at the bottom, making it resemble a boot—"GIMEL, YOU GET THE WHOLE POT. HAY"—again he pointed—"YOU GET HALF. AND SHIN"—another point—"YOU PUT ONE IN. ANY QUESTIONS?"

"Huh?" said Tasha. All the girls looked confused.

"JUST PLAY. IT'LL MAKE SENSE."

"Sufganiyot?" offered Jeremy, passing the platter.

"Ooooh!" My friends grabbed donuts, and my mom handed out cups of hot apple cider, each with a real cinnamon stick to use as a straw.

"You are so lucky, Zelly," said Jenny. Tasha and Talia nodded eagerly.

I stared at them. Were they making fun of me?

"Totally!" said Megan. "Jelly donuts for dinner and eight nights of presents? I want to be Jewish!"

"We also get gelt," said Jeremy. "Chocolate coins." He picked up a bag, pulled the net apart, stripped the foil wrapper from one, and popped it in his mouth.

Chocolate? *Oh no.* In a panic, I looked under the table to see that of all the dogs, only the puppy was still down there. I ran back to the living room, grabbed the bowls of candy off the coffee table, and moved them to a higher surface. Thankfully, Ace-the-dog was nowhere to be found and the bowls appeared to be untouched. From the kitchen, I could hear laughter and Ace-the-grandpa's loud voice, exclaiming over something.

I went to the doorway and peeked back in, feeling like Bubbles looking down from her cloud. The kitchen smelled all cinnamon-cozy. Jenny was scooping applesauce onto her potato pancake. Jeremy was showing off his master dreidel spin. Tasha was sneaking another jelly donut, while Talia had sucked all the jelly out of hers and left the deflated shell on her plate. Mrs. Stanley was talking to Mrs. Wright, my mom was carrying around plates of latkes, and Paul's dad seemed to have been drafted into grating potatoes now that Ace was leading the dreidel game.

So much for my perfect sleepover party.

With just me and my friends.

And yet.

There were no seats left, but Allie scooched over and

made room on her chair for me. Jeremy cupped his hands, whispered something to the dreidel inside, then snapped a spin decisively, sending the top whirling across the table so fast it flew off the other side and disappeared. Several of us bent under the table to see how it landed.

"Shin!" crowed Jenny. "That's shin, right? That means you have to put one in!"

"Interference!" howled Jeremy.

"Nuh-uh," said Megan. "You didn't let me have a do-over when mine fell. Fair's fair."

"Thanks," said Allie, accepting the dreidel from Mrs. Stanley, who had retrieved it from the floor.

Allie positioned the top carefully, but each time it wobbled rather than actually spinning. "Here, let me," I said. I took the dreidel and gave it a spin. Everyone watched as it whirled and twirled and landed on—

"Gimel!" yelled Jenny.

"CLOSE BUT NO CIGAR," said Ace.

"That's a nun," said Jeremy. "See—no heel."

"Man," complained Allie. "Here." She picked up the dreidel and handed it to Megan. "Your turn."

"What about Dreidel?" said Mrs. Stanley meaningfully to Mr. Stanley.

"Dreidel?" he said dubiously. *"Dreidel Stanley?"* Mrs. Stanley shot him a look. "Oh, all right, we can add it to the list. What do you think?" he asked the puppy in his arms. But she was already fast asleep.

"You know, Hanukkah is really different than I thought it would be," said Jenny.

"How so?" asked my mom.

"Well, I always thought you lit candles on Hanukkah. I didn't know you just put them in the candleholder."

My mom looked startled. Then she and my dad started to laugh. Jeremy and I joined them.

"I'm sorry," said Mom. "With this whole impromptu latke party, we completely forgot to light the candles in the first place." We gathered around and watched as she lit the shammes.

"Baruch atah Adonai . . . ," my parents, Sam, Jeremy, and I sang. Since Ace was singing too, it sounded more like "BARUCH ATAH ADONAI . . . !" But Ace wasn't done yet. He added one last bit for good measure, saying:

"BARUCH ATAH ADONAI, HAZAN ET HAKOL."

"That was beautiful," announced Mrs. Wright. "What does it mean?"

"IT'S A WAY OF GIVING THANKS," said Ace. "FOR LIGHT, AND FRIENDS, AND THE OTHER THINGS THAT SUSTAIN US. THROUGH GOOD TIMES AND NOT SO GOOD."

"Happy Hanukkah," said my dad, kissing me and Sam on the head. I gave him a hug, and over his shoulder I saw Ace squeeze Mrs. Wright's hand. I smiled without even checking with Bubbles on her cloud. I knew she'd say it was okay too.

By now, the kitchen was a complete mess. My perfect slumber party had turned into a crazy tzimmes of old people and misbehaving dogs and little boys running around covered with jam and sugar. There were greasy paper towels and foil chocolate wrappers, and nothing was cute or clean or at all the way I had wanted it.

And yet everybody was laughing. And eating. And playing dreidel. Lucky? Me?

Megan twisted the dreidel and gave it a spin. It landed on . . .

"Gimel?" she asked, pointing. "Right?"

Ace nodded, confirming.

"Woo-hooo!" yelled Megan. "Come to mama!" She raked the pile of coins toward herself. It was probably seventy-five cents, tops, but she acted like she had just become a millionaire.

"Don't get so comfortable, Miss Moneybags," I told her. "The change is just for playing with, not for keeps. It's from my tzedakah jug," I informed Jeremy.

"Sadako?" said Tasha.

"That Japanese girl with the paper cranes?" asked Talia.

"What?" said my mom.

"Actually—" Jeremy started to say.

"EXACTLY," interrupted Ace, with his definitive, judicial, all-argument-stopping voice of authority.

The kitchen was warm and cinnamony as the snow outside fell and fell. It was like being in a cozy bubble—an inside-out snow globe. I was surrounded by people who looked like they'd rather be right there than just about any place in the world. For the first time since I'd moved to Vermont, I felt lucky. I felt like I was home.

And my dog, my lovable, wonderful dog, came charging

into the kitchen chasing Rosie with something red and white hanging off both of his floppy ears like a pair of dangling earrings.

"What in the world?" I grabbed him by the collar and reached down to try to figure out whatever it was. I extracted a very sticky, very hairy half . . .

. . . of the giant candy cane that Allie had brought.

"Ace!!" I scolded.

"WHAT'D I DO?"

"Nothing, Grandpa," I told him, putting a hand on his shoulder. "You're fine. You're perfect."

And I meant it. Both Aces in my life were completely, ridiculously, perfectly themselves. Perfectly *Ace*. And, for once, that felt okay. Maybe not a total gimel, but definitely a hay.

Ace beamed and winked at me.

Two seconds later, he was all business.

"ALL RIGHT, WHO'S IN? ANTE UP."

TRAINING YOUR PUPPY

by Zelly Fried

First of all, if you want to get a dog (or even a cat or a guinea pig!), you should go to your local animal shelter, animal welfare league, or animal rescue group. There are lots of pets that need homes, and in my opinion mixed-breed dogs are the *best* dogs. They are super-smart and extra-cute and have their own personalities. Also, if you adopt a dog that is over a year old, it probably won't pee inside your house as much as a puppy, which is a very good thing as far as parents are concerned!

What you need to do next is take a dog-training class. Many of them let kids ten and up train their dogs as long as a grown-up will come to class with them. To find a class near you, contact your local animal shelter or animal welfare league or ask your veterinarian. Some animal shelters also have special camps (like Camp Paw Paw at the Humane Society of Chittenden County, in South Burlington, Vermont) for kids who are interested in learning more about animal care, training, and welfare.

The bottom line is this: If you put in the time to train,

and are positive and consistent, your puppy will learn to behave better, sooner or later. If you don't train your puppy, it is harder for your puppy, and you, and your parents—and harder on pretty much everything in your house, like shoes, books, and rugs. Trust me, I know! Ultimately, your success depends on two things: your puppy and *you*.

Here are some important training terms:

association – A connection between two different things. It's important to help your dog make associations between training and rewards like treats, praise, and attention from you.

break – A dog who doesn't wait to be released by his trainer is breaking the command. For example, if I told Ace to stay and I left the room, he would most likely break his stay before I returned and released him from it.

conditioning – Getting a dog used to something or to doing or not doing something—like not jumping up when greeting people.

handling – Working with your dog to teach him behaviors is called handling, and the people who train and show dogs in obedience competitions are called handlers.

marking – Doing something like providing a treat, praise, or a clicking sound to signal to a dog that he did the right thing. This immediate response marks the behavior and tells the dog, *Great job!*

recall – Getting your dog to come when called—ideally, the first time!

reinforcement – Sending a message to your dog. Positive reinforcement is best, because it tells your dog, *Yes!! Do more of that!*

release – Giving the dog a command to let him know that he is released from the obligation to keep doing what you commanded him to do. For example, after commanding "stay," you need to release the dog with a command like "okay."

repetition – It's how you get to Carnegie Hall! Practice makes perfect, so do it again and again and again. Repetition is the key to training a dog.

treats – Yummy small snacks provided to your dog as rewards during training!

YIDDISH GLOSSARY

by Zelly Fried (with a bissel help from Abraham "Ace" Diamond, her grandfather)

bissel – A little bit of something—often, but not always, food. My grandma used to say "Nem a bissel," which means "Take a little bite" or "Have a little taste." In other words, eat some!

bupkis – Nothing.

dreidel – From the Yiddish word *dreyen* ("to spin or turn") it basically means "a little spinning thing." Which is exactly what it is.

facacta – Stupid and ridiculous.

feh – Yuck. Not to be confused with *meh*, which means "not terrible, but not so terrific, either."

finagle – This word sounds Yiddish, but my grandpa insists that, technically, it isn't. It means "to get what you want by tricking someone or bending the rules." But I think my grandpa says it to mean "to work the system."

fress – To wolf down food. One who does so is a fresser.

For example, "Ace, don't be such a fresser. Chew that dog biscuit before swallowing it."

gedaingst – Remember. As in: "I told you I knew what I was doing, gedaingst?"

gelt – Money or coins (real or chocolate—yum!).

kipa – The Hebrew word for *yarmulke*, which is Yiddish. Both words are for the flat cap that some Jewish people (like Jeremy) wear some of the time and some Jewish people wear all of the time (and some, like me, don't wear at all).

kugel – A food that's somewhere between a pudding and a casserole. It's made with either noodles (noodle kugel) or potatoes (potato kugel) and a lot of other stuff to hold it together. Kugel comes in other flavors, too—apple, zucchini, you name it. Ace says there are as many different kinds of kugel as there are fish in the sea, but as far as I know, there's no such thing as fish kugel.

kvetch – To complain, often repetitively. Someone who does this—no names mentioned—is a kvetch, though of course he would never admit to it.

latkes - Delicious potato pancakes fried in oil and often served at Hanukkah (to commemorate the miraculous oil that lasted for eight nights).

mazel tov – I always thought this was just the Hebrew phrase for congratulations, but my grandpa says it originally came from Yiddish. *Tov* means "good" in both languages, and *mazel* is the Yiddish word for "fortune" or "luck." Remember that when I get to the word *schlimazel*!

megilla – A long detailed story.

mensch – A good person, someone you can really count on to do the right thing. Often, mensches are also kind of dorky, but that's okay too.

meshuggener, meshugge – A crazy person is a meshuggener, and a crazy thing (or dog) is meshugge.

mishegoss – This comes from the same word as *meshuggener* and *meshugge* do and it sort of means "craziness," though it is more like "nuttiness" or "wackiness."

nosh – It means "snack" and it also means "to snack." So you can nosh on a nosh!

nu – This means something like "So?" or "Well?" But my grandpa says "So nu?" which seems redundant to me, but I would never try telling him that.

oy vey, vey iz mir – *Oy vey* is like "oh no," and *vey iz mir* is like an *oy vey* with extra oomph!

pisher – This actually means "someone who pees"! No wonder my grandpa says it to my dog so much. But it also means "a little kid" or "a little guy."

potchke – Ace says this means "to make a mess" or "to do something carelessly." *Potch* means "slap," so it kind of means "to do something in a slapdash way." But I think of it as meaning "fiddle with" because my mom tells Sam not to potchke with things like the locks on the car doors.

rugelach – "Little corners" or "little twists" of dough made with sour cream, cinnamon, and often filled with chocolate, or jam. Bubbles made the best rugelach. They were delicious!

schlemiel – A fool or an idiot—not to be confused with a schlimazel.

schlep – To drag something. For example, my brother, Sam, schlepped his dirty old stuffed whale around with him everywhere until my mother made him stop.

schlimazel – A super-unlucky person. As Ace explains it, "A schlemiel is a guy who spills his soup—onto a schlimazel's lap." Remember how I said *mazel tov* means "good luck"? The *mazel* in *schlimazel* also means "luck"—but it is the *other* kind of luck!

schmaltz – Chicken fat, which should be thrown out, if you ask me. Or spread on toast, if you ask my grandpa. *Schmaltzy* is a word I've heard my parents use to describe extra-corny or sappy movies, songs, or decorations. I have no idea why.

schmatte – A rag or something that used to be nice but is completely worn out and has turned into a rag. For example, a stuffed whale that you schlep around soon becomes a schmatte.

schtickl – A little piece of something, usually something good to eat. From what I can tell, a schtickl is bigger than a bissel, but not by much.

sha – It's sort of like "Shhh!" You say it to tell someone to hush or be quiet.

shammes – This means "helper," and that's why you call the Hanukkah candle you use to help light all the other candles the shammes.

shivah – Meaning "seven" in Hebrew, this is what you call the week after someone in your close family dies. When Bubbles, my grandma, died, lots of people came to visit while we sat shivah. Almost all of them brought food—mostly danishes and deli platters.

shvitz – A steam bath or sauna where people would get together and sweat a lot in the olden days.

sufganiyot – Jelly donuts fried in oil and served at Hanukkah. Like latkes, these are traditional because of the story of the oil lasting eight nights. Works for me!

tchotchke – A little toy or collectible. You keep tchotchkes on a tchotchke shelf.

tuches – Put it this way: if someone gave you a potch in tuches, it would hurt to sit down afterward. Yup, you guessed it!

tzedakah – Charity, but it doesn't mean *just* that. It also sort of means "helping your community." Ace says it's not only what you do for other people, but it's how you do it. He calls it "the most important seasoning." He also says the three keys to happiness are love, tzedakah, and prunes. I'm not sure I agree with that one hundred percent, but who am I to argue with him?

ACKNOWLEDGMENTS

First, let me express my appreciation to grandparents everywhere, especially the truly *great* grandparents (and *fabulous* great-aunts and great-uncles) my kids are (and have been) lucky enough to have in their lives. You inspire me in so many ways, though I promise that the part in the book you are pointing at is *definitely* not you.

Thanks to Erin Clarke, Nancy Hinkel, and the wonderful team at Knopf, as well as Carrie Hannigan and the terrific team at HSG, for giving me the opportunity and the encouragement to keep going with Zelly and Ace. Thanks to Lisa Schamberg, Pat Robins, and Mr. Chuckles, who provided me with the Vermont residency at which this book first took shape. Thanks also to the Virginia Center for the Creative Arts for supporting my work as that shape evolved . . . and evolved. And thanks to Mike, Franny, and Bougie for being the wonderful people that they are and for releasing me to go write when they would have preferred not to.

Thanks to the Association of Jewish Libraries, the Jewish Book Council, and all of the educators, librarians, media specialists, booksellers, bloggers, rabbis, and friends old and new who helped share *When Life Gives You O.J.* with readers. Thanks especially to Johnny Orangeseed and everyone who went the extra mile for *O.J.* I won't list all of you because I will inevitably forget someone and feel truly awful, but you know who you are and I hope you know how much I appreciate you. Thanks also to all of the kids (and classes and book clubs) who were moved to create their own practice pets—you guys rock! Please keep sending photos (oj@ericaperl.com) and keep up the hard work. I have no doubt your parents are noticing how dedicated you are.

Thanks to the Humane Society of Chittenden County (especially Gina Berk and Camp Paw Paw!), the Washington Animal Rescue League, and Lucky Dog Animal Rescue. Thanks also to Shannon Hall and the Capital Dog Training Club, Dr. Jay Merker and Collins Animal Hospital, and Dr. Solomon Perl. Special thanks to Maggie, Lucy, and Clover for their unconditional devotion, as well as for plenty of material.

Thank you to everyone at First Book for being great friends to me and my books, as well as for tirelessly and with great humor providing millions of books to children in need every year (firstbook.org). Thanks especially to Kyle, Jane, and Chandler for bringing me on board in the first place *because* I had a chicken hat, not despite it.

Most importantly, thanks to my husband, Mike Sewell. Thank you for what you said that night at New York Noodletown, and for showing you meant it every day since. I love you with all my heart. And not just because you look great mowing the lawn.

Michael Sewell

Erica S. Perl

is the author of *When Life Gives You O.J.*, *Vintage Veronica*, and a number of picture books, including the well-loved *Chicken Butt!* books. Erica was raised in Burlington, Vermont, by transplanted New Yorkers. She currently lives in Washington, D.C., with her husband, two daughters, and their amazing dog, Clover. Learn more about Erica and her books at EricaPerl.com.